The Collected Poetry of **Langston Hughes** In English & Japanese

ラングストン・ヒューズ 英日選詩集

友愛
For Brotherly Love

・

自由
Freedom

・

夢屑
Dream Dust

・

霊歌
and **Spirituals**

水崎 野里子
翻訳

Translated by
Noriko Mizusaki

コールサック社

Coal Sack
Publishing Company

ラングストン・ヒューズ 英日選詩集

友愛・自由・夢屑・霊歌

水崎野里子 訳

I

友愛

アメリカを　再びアメリカに

アメリカよ　再びアメリカであれ
かつての　夢のアメリカに
かつて　草原の開拓者が　夢見たアメリカ
自由の国　アメリカに

（アメリカは私にはアメリカであったことはない）

アメリカよ　その夢となれ　彼らが夢見た夢の国に
偉大なる　強靱な愛の地
神によって潰されるべき
悪と共謀する王も　独裁者の陰謀もない

8

（アメリカは私にはアメリカであったことはない）

おお　私の国よ　自由の地となれ
自由が　真の愛国の　王の冠を戴く国
機会均等の実現　差別のない暮らし
平等は　我々が呼吸する大気の中にあれ

（私に平等はなかった
自由もなかった　この「自由の国」で）

「言え　誰だおまえは？　暗闇の中でぶつくさ言っている奴は？
おまえは誰だ？　星々を闇で覆い隠す奴は？」

私は貧しい白人（ファー・ホワイト）だ　馬鹿にされ　のけ者だ
私はアフロ系だ　奴隷の傷跡を背負っている

9

私は赤い男だ　俺たちの地から追われた
私は移民だ　希望を求め　希望にしがみついている――
その結果　いつも変わらないくだらない足枷
共食い　弱肉強食

私は若い男だ　力と希望に溢れているが
相も変わらぬ　果てしのない鎖でがんじがらめ
利益　権力　儲けの鎖　奴らは　土地を握る！
金を握る！　必用品を満足に得る道を握る！
仲間を働かせる！　賃金を略奪する！
強欲で　すべてを手に入れる！　その鎖

私は農夫　土に縛られている
私は労働者　機械に売られた
私はアフロ系　お前たちすべての召使

私は　おごらず　腹を空かせ　貧しき者――
アメリカの夢にもかかわらず　今日　空腹だ
今日　殴られた――おお　開拓者たち！
私は　夢を叶えたことは一度もない
年中打ちのめされている　貧しい労働者

だが私は　そのアメリカの夢を夢見た者
旧世界で　いまだ王たちの奴隷だった頃
夢を見た　とても強く　勇敢で　真実の夢
あらゆる石や煉瓦の中で　掘り返された畑の中で
それは今でも　力強く　勇気ある歌と聞こえる
それはアメリカを今のアメリカとなした基礎だった
おお　私はかつて　昔　海を渡った者
私の本国だと願う国を探して――
私は暗いアイルランドの岸辺を去り

11

ポーランドの草原　イギリスの草地を過ぎ

アフリカの岸辺から引き剥がされて　私は来た

「自由の国」を建国するために

アメリカの自由？

誰がアメリカの自由と言った？　私は言わなかったか？

たしかに私は言わなかったか？　幾百万の人々はやすらかに信じている？

抗議して幾百万の人々は打ち殺された？

私たちは支払ったのに　幾百万の人々は何も得てはいない？

すべての夢を　私たちは夢見た

すべての歌を　私たちは歌った

すべての希望を　私たちは抱いた

すべての旗を　私たちは掲げた

私たちの支払いにもかかわらず　人々は何も得ていない──

アメリカの夢だけ　だがそれは　今日では死んだも同然だ

おお　アメリカ　アメリカを再びアメリカとなせ——
アメリカ　自由の国では一度もあり得なかった国——
だが　あらゆる人々が自由でなければならない国——アメリカ
私の国——貧しい人々　ネイティヴアメリカンの　私　アフロ系の国——
私たちがアメリカを作った
私たちの汗と血　信仰と痛み
鋳物工場での手　雨の中の耕作
それらはきっと力強い夢を再び私たちにもたらしてくれる

呼べ　私を　いかなる醜い名前でもいい　あなたたちが好むなら——
鋼鉄の自由は汚れはしない
人々の生命に蛭のように住み付く輩から
私たちは　私たちの国を取り戻すのだ

アメリカ！

おお　そうだ

嘘は言わない

アメリカは一度もアメリカではなかった　私には

でも　私は誓う——

アメリカは自由の国になるだろう！

やくざ者の死の荒廃と廃墟から

レイプと賄賂の腐敗、窃盗、嘘から

私たち　アメリカの人民は　取り戻すのだ

国を　鉱脈を　植物を　河を

山々を　広大な草原を——

すべてを　広大な緑の国土のすべての拡がりを——

再び　アメリカを作りましょう！

14

自由の鋤

われらが　無から始めようとすれば

何も持たない　汚れていない手で

始めようとすれば

世界の構築を始めれば

最初は　ひとりで始める

心の中の　信仰と共に──

強さは　そこにある

意志は　そこにある　世界を構築しよう

最初は　夢でしかない

それから　道を探し始める

彼は　世界を発見する
偉大な森の世界を
世界の豊かな土壌を
世界の幾多の川を

彼は見る　そこに　構築の材料を
幾多の困難もまた　障害も
手は探す　木を伐る道具を
土を耕し　水力を利用する器具を
それから　助けてくれる他者の手を探す
助力の人々の手の共同体を――
そうすれば　夢はひとりの男だけの夢ではなくなる
共同体の夢になる
私の夢ではなく　私たちの夢になるのだ
私だけの世界ではなく

16

君の世界と私の世界になる

構築するすべての手に属する　世界に

かつて　だが大昔ではない

船が海を渡って来た

ピルグリムたちや祈祷師を乗せて[*1]

冒険家や戦利品目当ての者たちも乗せて

自由民と年季奉公の召使

奴隷たち　奴隷の主人　すべて新たなる世界

新世界アメリカへ！

帆を風で膨らませ　ガレオン船[*2]はやって来た

男たちと夢を運んだ　女たちと夢を運んだ

小さな共同体を作り　一緒に

17

心を通わせ
手を差し伸べ合い
アメリカの建設を始めた
自由の手を持つ者たちは
より大きな自由を求め
年季契約の者の手は
彼らなりの自由を願った
奴隷である者たちの手は
心の中の　自由の種を護り続けた
自由という言葉はいつも　存在し続けた

　　　　　自由

大地の中へと　自由の鋤は食い込んだ
自由民の手に　奴隷たちの手に　握られて
使用人の手に　冒険家の手に握られ
鋤は　豊かな土を耕した　多くの者に握られて

そこに　食糧の苗が植えられ　収穫された

木綿は　アメリカに衣服を着せた

多数の者の手に握られ　斧は木を伐った

木材は切り刻まれ　アメリカの屋根を作った

多くの河や海に乗り入れ　飛沫を上げ

船は　アメリカの輸送手段となった

馬を追う鞭の音は　アメリカの草原に響き渡った

自由の手　奴隷の手　使用人の手　冒険家の手

白い手とアフロ系の手は

鋤を握り

斧を　ハンマーを握った

船を進ませ　馬を鞭打った

食糧を作り　家を作り　船で輸送した

共に力を合わせ　労働によって

皆の手が　アメリカを作った

労働！　労働によって　村が出来た

村は街となり　街は市となった

労働！　労働によって　漕ぎ船が作られ

帆船が作られ　蒸気船が作られ

荷馬車が作られ　駅馬車となった

労働によって　工場が作られ　鋳物工場や鉄道

店が　市場が　店舗が　商店が　作られた

強固な製品は　型に入れられ　製造され

商店で売られた　倉庫に積まれ　世界中に送られた

労働によって――白い手もアフロ系の手も――

共に　夢を　力を　願いを実現し

アメリカを築いた

今　私はここにいる　あなたは　そこ

今　マンハッタン　シカゴ

シアトル　ニューオーリンズ

今　アメリカ合衆国

ボストン　エル・パソ

ひとりの男が言った

かつて　だがそんなに大昔ではない時

　　すべて人間は　創られた

　平等に……

　　創造主により

　　与えられた

　　奪うことが

　　出来ない

　　権利である……

　　　この生活の中の

21

人々の解放　そして
　　　幸福の追求

彼の名前はジェファーソン[3]
当時は　まだ奴隷たちはいた
でも　奴隷たちもまた彼を信頼した
沈黙のうちに　彼らは
ジェファーソンの述べたことは
同じく　自分たちにも当然のことと考えた
そして　やがて
リンカーン[4]は言った

　　どんな人間も他者を
　　支配してはならない

その他者の合意

なしには

当時奴隷もいた
でも心の中で　奴隷たちは　リンカーンの言が
あらゆる人間にあてはまると理解した――
そうでなければ　誰にとっても意味がなかった
そしてある男は言った

　　奴隷として生きるより
　　死んで自由になる方がましだ

彼はアフロ系であり奴隷であった
でも　逃げ出して自由になった
奴隷たちは知っていた

フレディック・ダグラスの言は正しいと *5
ハーパーズフェリーでジョン・ブラウンと共に *6
アフロ系の人々は死んだ
ジョン・ブラウンは死刑になった
南北戦争以前　時代は暗かった
誰にもまるでわからなかった
いつ自由が勝利するかを
「あてにならんな」と思う者もいた

だが　他の者たちは自由の勝利を疑わなかった
奴隷制度の暗黒の時代に
心の中で自由の種を護りながら
奴隷たちは歌を作った

鋤を手で握り

続けよ

　　　握り続けよ！

自由はやって来る！

握り続けよ！

歌はまさに言う通りだ

　　　握り続けよ！

　　　　続けよ！

　　　　鋤を手で握り

戦争で　自由は来た　多くの血が流された

恐ろしいほどに

だが　自由は来た！

いつものように　当時　疑う者もいた

25

南北戦争は確かに終わったか

奴隷は自由になったか

連邦の統一は保たれたか

だが　今　我々は知る　すべては成就した

人民にも国家にも　暗黒の時代から

自由は成就した

戦闘の雲が晴れた時　光があった

偉大な森の大地があり

人民は　ひとつの国家に合一した

アメリカは夢だ

詩人は言う　それは約束だった

ホワイトの人々は言う　それは約束だ──だが

未来に実現するだろうと

彼らは常に　物事を声をあげて言うとは限らない

紙にはっきりと書き記すこともない

彼らは　しばしば　持ち続ける

心の奥底で　偉大な考えを

だが　しばしば　表現が間違っており

途切れ途切れ　つまずきながら言う

そして　間違いのあるまま　実行に移す

彼らは　互いに　理解も出来ない

でも　どこかそこに

いつも理解しようとする努力があり

そういう人々は言う

「君は人間だ　一緒に私たちの国

を築こう」

アメリカ！

共に創られた国

27

共に育てた夢

鋤を手に握り続けよ！　離すな！

もし　家がまだ　未完成でも

気落ちするな　建築者よ！

もし　戦闘がいまだ　勝利ではなくても

負けるな　兵士よ！

図と　型紙はここにある

はじめから　織られている

アメリカという　ゆがんだ織物に

すべての人々は創られた

平等に

誰も　他者を

支配しては

ならない　同意なしには

奴隷として生きるより
死んだほうがましだ

誰がそう言った？　アメリカ人だ！
誰の所有だ？　アメリカだ！
アメリカとは誰だ？　君だ　私だ！
我々は　アメリカだ！
外部から　我々を征服する敵には
我々は言う　だめだ！
内部から　我々を征服し分割する敵には
我々は言う　だめだ！

自由
　友愛
　　民主主義！

これらの偉大な言葉に反逆する敵には
我々は言う　だめだ！

歌を作った
奴隷とされた人々は　自由に向かいながら

昔のことだ

　　鋤を手で握れ！
　　　離すな！

その鋤は　新しい畝溝を耕した
歴史の畑を横切った
その溝の中に自由の種は落とされた

その種から一本の木が育った　育っている
永遠に育つだろう
その木は　皆のための木だ
アメリカすべての　全世界のための
その枝は拡がり　木陰は大きくなり
すべての人種とすべての人々が知り木陰で集う

　　　鍬を手で
　　握れ！
　握り続けよ！

31

＊1　正確にはピルグリム・ファーザーズと俗に呼ばれる。一六二〇年、信仰の自由（新教）を求めてメイフラワー号に乗りイギリスのサザンプトン港から出発し、アメリカのマサチューセッツ州プリマスに上陸、入植した。それよりも十二年前に同じく宗教的な自由を求めてオランダのライデンに移住したイギリス分離派教会の三十五名を含め、総勢百二名を数え、彼らは清教徒（ピューリタン）と呼ばれる。アメリカの新教の基礎となった。ちなみに、彼らが初めての収穫を祝った日を感謝祭（サンクスギビングデー）と呼び、アメリカでは祝日となっている。十一月の第四木曜日に指定されている。当日は家族や友人で集まり、七面鳥（ターキー）を食べるのが習わしである。

＊2　ガレオン船とは十五世紀から十六世紀にかけて、大型の火砲、大砲の海上での発射に向けてイギリス（ヘンリー八世の時代）で考案された三〜四層甲板の大型帆船。軍艦と商船に使用された。以前はガレー船（主に地中海において三千年以上に渡って使用された船。オール・櫂で人間が漕ぐ大型船）であったが、大型の大砲の搭乗には一層甲板では無理があった。

＊3　トマス・ジェファーソン（一七四七―一八二六）。バージニア州出身。アメリカの十三の州によるアメリカ独立戦争（アメリカ革命とも言う。一七七五―一七八三）。ジェファーソンはアメリカ独立宣言を起草、一八七六年に独立宣言。なおアメリカ独立戦争の司令官はアメリカの初代大統領となったジョージ・ワシントンである。イギリスがアメリカ十三州の独立に署名したのは一七八三年であり、同時に、正式にアメリカ合衆国が建国された。ジェファーソンはやがて第三代アメリカ大統領。なお、アメリカ合衆国憲法は一七八七年

に作成され、一七八八年に発布。

*4 エイブラハム・リンカーン（一八〇九─一八六五）。第十六代アメリカ大統領。ケンタッキー州出身。アメリカの南北の軋轢の中で一八六〇年に大統領に当選。一八六一年には南北戦争が始まり、一八六三年に奴隷解放宣言を発布。翌年大統領選に再選。

*5 フレデリック・ダグラス（一八一八─一八九五）。メリーランド出身の元奴隷。奴隷制度廃止活動家、政治家（共和党）。ワシントンD.C.の自宅で逝去。奴隷であったころに彼に読み書きを教えた女主人がいた。やがて彼は奴隷の身分から脱出を図った。以降、「皮膚の色、性別を問わず、人はみな平等の権利を与えられるべきだ」をモットーに、奴隷解放を主張してアメリカ各地、イギリスやアイルランドを講演して回った。新聞も発行し、一八六三年、リンカーン大統領と黒人参政権について協議した。南北戦争後、解放奴隷救済銀行の総裁を務めた。

*6 ジョン・ブラウン（一八〇〇─一八五九）。コネチカット州生まれ、バージニア州チャールズタウン没。アメリカの奴隷廃止論者、奴隷解放運動家、フレデリック・ダグラス、エイブラハム・リンカーン、そして南北戦争の以前に生きた人物である。奴隷解放を主張し、カンザス州で奴隷制度賛成者五人を虐殺（ポタワトミー虐殺）。一八五九年にバージニアとメリーランドに逃亡奴隷のための本拠地建設を計画し、バージニア州のハーパーズフェリーにあった連邦武器庫を**襲撃**して逮捕され、処刑された。ブラウン蜂起と言われる。

33

友愛

南部の白い市民の方々へ
ささやかな手紙

私たちアフロ系が　モンゴメリーで抗議の列に入り[*]
彼らが　愛について教えている列に入り
私が手を差し伸べたら　どうか　受け止めてください——
それとも　切り捨て　問題を　神に委ねますか？

もしも　私が心から　あなた方を愛せると思えば
もしも　本当に愛せると思うなら
もしも　私が「兄弟　私はあなたを許します」と言えば
あなた方は　少しでも　聞いてくれますか？

34

長い　とても長い間　あなた方は呼んでいました
私を　あらゆる種類の名前で　私を抑え付けました
私は泳いで来ました　頭を深く　水の中に潜らせ
あなた方は望んだ　私がそこに居続けて　溺れて死ぬことを

それでもあなたたちは大騒ぎしたがる
「とにかく　私はあなたたちを愛しています」と答えても
怒っています　私は座りませんから　あなたがたのバスの一番後ろの席に
でも　私は死にませんでした　いまだに泳いでいます　あなたたちは　今

聞いて下さい　市民の方々！
モンゴメリーでキング師と共に列を組みます──
でも　聖書が述べることを私は実行します──
私はあなたたちを愛します──本当です　命を賭けて！

35

＊

アラバマ州の州都。アメリカ合衆国南部。この詩は一九五五年にモンゴメリーで起こった、アフロ系女性ローザ・パークスによる、モンゴメリー・バス・ボイコット事件に言及している。当時はアラバマ州モンゴメリー市ではアフロ系への人種分離法がいまだ残っており、バス前方は白人用の席、後部はアフロ系用の席と決められていた。バスが混んで白人用の席が足らなくなった時、座っていたアフロ系の乗客は席を立って白人に席を譲らなければならない慣習が出来ていた。運転手は境界を移動することが出来た。ローザは初めはアフロ系の席の最前列に座っていたが、バスが混んできたので運転手はローザに立つように命じた。だが、ローザは立たなかった。運転手は警察に通報し、ローザは逮捕された。一日拘置所に入れられたが即日保釈された。だがモンゴメリーの市役所内での州簡易裁判所で罰金刑を宣告される。

ローザ逮捕の知らせが伝わると、モンゴメリーのデクスター街バプテスト教会で牧師に就任したばかりだったマーティン・ルーサー・キング・ジュニア牧師（当時二十六歳）たちが抗議運動に立ち上がり、市内のアフロ系の人々に市営バス乗車を拒否する抗議行動を呼び掛けた。ローザ側はやがてバス車内の人種隔離の条例は違憲であると控訴、一九五六年十一月、連邦最高裁判所は人種隔離法に違憲の判決を出した。バス・ボイコット運動は三八一日間続いたが、連邦最高裁判決の翌日に収束した。ラングストン・ヒューズの本詩はこの時点で書かれている。

キング牧師はこの運動の勝利を機に全米各地で公民権運動を指揮し、非暴力行動と市民権主張の不服従を掲げ、一九六三年にワシントン大行進で二十五万人を集めた抗議集会を開催

する。そこでリンカーン記念堂前での師の演説、「私には夢がある」は歴史に残る名演説である。翌年一九六四年の公民権法成立に繋がった。一方、当時のアメリカ大統領ジョン・ケネディ政権は次々と南部諸州における差別制度を禁止する立法を実行した。ケネディを継いだリンドン・ジョンソン大統領政権もアフロ系の人々の社会的地位を積極的に向上させるために、「偉大なアメリカ」へ向かうべき肯定的措置（アファーマティヴ・アクション）の演説に始まり、ケネディ政権時代の差別撤廃の立法を促進させている。

ローザ・バークスとマーティン・ルーサー・キング牧師はアメリカにおける公民権運動（Civil Rights Movements）のアフロ系の活動家として現在、輝かしい名を残す。彼らの陰に、だがやはり詩人としてペンで差別と闘い、自由と平等を求めてアフロ系の人権と人間性を詩として書き続けたラングストン・ヒューズがいたことは明記すべきであろう。彼は生前に一九六四年の公民権法の実現を見た。一九二〇年代に始まる、アフロ系の人間性と霊歌、アフロ系ジャズ音楽を高揚、普及させたハーレム・ルネサンスの芸術運動からアフロ系市民権獲得運動まで——差別と分離政策の苦難にめげず、解放と自由と平等を求めて常に歌い続けて来た詩人がここにいる。

民主主義

民主主義は　来ないだろう

今日も　今年も

　永遠に

馴れ合いと　恐れによって

私は　権利を持つ

他の奴らと　同じほど

　立つ

二本足で

土地の所有

「物事は成り行きに任せろ」
「明日になれば　変わるだろう」
うんざりだ　人々がそう言うのを聞くのは
死んだら　自由は要らない
明日のパンでは生きられない

自由は
強い種だ
植えられた
大いなる必要性の中で
私もまたアメリカに住む
私は自由を望む
あなたと同じく

自
由

アメリカ難民

「自由」という言葉がある
言ってごらん　なんと　素晴らしい
私は心の竪琴で　自由の歌を歌う
一日中　毎日

「解放」という言葉がある
聞けば　泣きたくなる
私の知ったことを　あなたも知っていたら
あなたもきっと　なぜだかわかる

ジョージアの黄昏

暗闇が隠すものを　ヴェールで覆う
孤独で　哀しい　ジョージアの黄昏
泣いて　泣いて　泣きまくる
時々　風がある　ジョージアの黄昏には

誰の血だ?　……みんなのさ
深紅のしたたり　ジョージアの黄昏に
太陽光線が残して行った　ジョージアの黄昏
時々　血痕がある　ジョージアの黄昏

＊　ジョージアとはアメリカ南部の州。首都はアトランタ。

43

ハーレム

何が起こるんだ？　今まで言えなかった夢を今言うのかい？

干からびている？
陽に照らされた　干しブドウみたいに？
それとも
膿爛れた傷のように　痛いの？
それから　走って逃げる？
腐った肉みたいに　悪臭がする？
それとも　甘ったるい菓子みたいに？
パンの耳に砂糖をまぶした？──

多分　ちょっと息切れ

重い荷物を背負って

あるいは　爆発？

ニューヨークの人々

私はここで生まれた

嘘じゃない　おやじはそう言った

ここだ　神の空の下だ

私が生まれたのは　ここじゃない　おふくろは言った

私はここに来た――なぜ？

私の生まれたところでは

アフロ系は懸命に働く

生きている間はずっと

死ぬまで

決して　場所を所有することはない

大地にも空にも
だから　私はここに来た
今　私は　何を持つ？
　　あなたよ！

彼女の唇　天に昇った
暗闇の中
同じく古い　火花！

星

ハーレムの街の上　星が流れ去る

夜　忘却の　小さな息
街のビルディング
母の歌
街は夢見る
子守歌

手を差し伸べよ　アフロ系(ダークボーイ)の少年よ
星を摑むんだ
忘却の　小さな息から
それは　夜

48

星を
摑め

ジム・クロウ列車でのランチ[*]

君の夢から　弁当箱を取り出したまえ

君の心臓のサンドイッチを嚙み続けよ

そしてジム・クロウ列車に乗り続けよ

最後にそいつが金切声を上げるまで　それから――

原子爆弾みたいに――ばらばらに爆発するまで

　　＊　アフロ系と白人の客車が分かれている列車、今は撤廃されている。

片道切符

私の人生を　持ち上げ
一緒に　連れて行く
そして　置く

シカゴで　デトロイトで
バッファローで　スクラントンで
どこでも　いい
北部と東部なら
南部の州はだめ

私の人生を　持ち上げ
一緒に　汽車に乗る

ロサンジェルスへ　ベイカーズフィールド

シアトル　オークランド　ソルトレイクへ

どこでも　いい

北部と東部なら

南部は抜き

飽き飽きだ

人種隔離法は

人々は残酷で

恐れている

リンチして　逃げる

私を怖がる

私は　怖い

私の人生を　持ち上げ

運んで行く
片道切符で――
北部へ行って　帰らない
西部へ出かけて　帰らない
行ったきり

自由列車

私は読んだ　新聞で
　自由列車について
私は聞いた　ラジオで
　自由列車について
私は見た　人々が語り合うのを
　自由列車について
主よ　私はずっと待ち続けている
　自由列車！

アメリカ南部の諸州を走る唯一の列車　私の夢
隔離車両は*　撤廃

隔離車両なんて　ないほうがいいな　自由列車には
裏口ドアなどない　自由列車には
ホワイトだけとは書いてない　自由列車には

　　　乗ってみたいな　この
　　　自由列車

誰が　自由列車の機関士ですか？
石炭みたいな真っ黒い男が　運転出来る？　自由列車を？
それとも私は　いまだ門番　自由列車では？
投票箱はありますか？　自由列車には？
ミシシッピで停まる時　ちゃんとはっきり書いてある？
自由列車に　誰もが乗る権利があると？

　　　誰かが　私に話してくれた　この

55

自由列車！

バーミンガム駅には印があった　カラードあっち　ホワイトこっちと
ホワイト乗客　左行く　有色乗客　右へ行け――
道も別々　分離
そんな風に自由列車にも乗るのかな？

　　私は知りたい　この
　　自由列車

もしも　私の子供たちが「おとうさん　教えてよ
なぜ　隔離駅が自由列車にあるの？」と訊いて来たら
なんと答えたらいいのかな？――教えてください
なぜならば　自由は自由ではありません
人間が自由でないかぎり

56

でもおそらくは彼らが説明してくれるでしょう

自由列車に乗れば

お前たちここに用はない！」

ホワイト男は怒鳴ります「帰れ！

彼女が自由列車を見ようと並んでいれば

八十三歳でアフロ系

アトランタにいる私のおばあちゃんは

　　「すみません　私は　これは自由列車と

　　　思ったのです」

彼女の孫の名前はジミー

彼は死にました　頭にきて

彼は死んだ　本当です　誰にも知らされませんでした
彼らがこの自由列車で運んでいた自由は
本物でしたか？　あるいはまた　見せかけだけ？

　　ジミーは知りたい
　　自由列車とは？

ジミーの自由列車は　太陽の光に輝きながら
線路を疾走　ホワイトにもアフロ系にも？
カラードとかホワイトとか　区別なし
真昼の光が照る　野原の中で停車するだけ
広々とした田舎の中で停車する
そこではどこにも人種隔離表示などありません
歓迎委員会とか　お偉い政治家とか

市長とか　アフロ系が投票できないそんな方々はいない

人種隔離の印なし――

自由列車は　あなたの列車　私の列車！

アメリカで　君たちの列車　私の列車！

アフロ系もホワイトも言う「ナイスだよ！」

米軍兵士は「俺たちそいつを願ってた！」

墓の中から言うでしょう

そうしたら　おそらく　〝頭にきて〟死んだ者たちは

私は叫びます　「自由列車に栄光あれ！」と

大声で叫びます　「汽笛を鳴らせ　自由列車！」と

全能なる神よ　感謝します！

自由列車　ここにあり！

自由列車に　いざ　乗りましょう！

＊ 原語はジム・クロウ法車両。南北戦争後、一八七六年から一九六四年にかけて存在した、人種差別・隔離を含むアメリカ合衆国南部諸州や西海岸の州法の総称。病院、バス、電車、レストラン、結婚、学校、などに渡る、かつてのカラード・アフロ系への隔離政策。

船乗り

彼は座っていた　揺れる甲板に
故郷から　世界半分　離れた
巻き煙草をふかし　見つめていた
青い波　泡の王冠

彼は人魚を抱いていた
胸の前に　しっかりと
背中には　イレズミ
青い鳥は　巣の中

リンカーン劇場*

リンカーンの頭が　壁から見下ろしている
映画はこだまする　スクリーン上のドラマ
リンカーンの頭は　清らかに高い
映画を　おとなしく見ている
アフロ系の人々の一群　その上方で
映画は終わる　ぎらつく明かりが灯される
下方のボックスで　バンドが突然　ジャズの演奏
彼らは拍手する　太った　褐色の肌の女に　髪は
漂白した金髪　彼女は歌う　よくある女の失恋の歌
指をパチンと鳴らし　ゆっくりと腰を振り
泣きながら　赤く塗った唇　派手で相応しくない印象

62

「あたしの恋人　あたしを捨てた　悲しくて」

金持のホワイトの衣類を毎日洗う少女たち

愛をコインで取引する　髪をなめらかに撫でつけた少年たちは

共に手を握り合い　彼女の歌に笑いこけた

　＊

　リンカーン劇場とは南北戦争（一八六一―一八六五）中に奴隷解放宣言を宣言し（一八六二年九月二十二日）公布（翌年一月一日より）した第十六代アメリカ大統領アブラハム・リンカーン（一八〇九―一八六五）が観劇中に狙撃された劇場で、正式名はフォード劇場という。地下にリンカーン博物館がある。狙撃後リンカーンが運ばれたと言われる道路向かいのピーターセンハウスと共にフォード劇場の地下にある博物館は現在、リンカーン博物館として一般公開されている。共にワシントンD・C・の国立公園内にある。リンカーンは一八六五年四月十四日、フォード劇場のボックス席で夫人やヘンリー・ラズボーン少佐等四人で観劇していた最中、俳優のジョン・ウィルクス・ブースがボックス席に侵入、後頭部を至近距離から撃たれた。大統領は道路向かいのピーターセンハウスに運ばれたが、死亡。遺体は一時、同じ公園内にある国会議事堂に安置された。議事堂内には現在、リンカーンの座像が据えられている。なお、リンカーンとの呼称は日本語呼称であり、英語ではリンコン（Lincoln）とも発音する。

63

私もまた　アメリカを歌う

私は　ダークの兄弟だ
彼らは　仲間が来ると
私に　台所へ行って食事しろと言う
でも　私は笑う
そして　快適に食べる
そして　強くなる

明日
私は　同じテーブルに座るだろう
彼らが来ても
誰も　言わないだろう

「台所で食え」とは

彼らは見るだろう　なんと私は美しいか
そして　　恥ずかしがりやだか――

私もまた　アメリカを歌う

アラバマの夜明け

もし作曲家になれたなら
書きたい曲は
アラバマの夜明け
そして素敵な歌付ける
沼地の霧のように立ち上がる
やさしい露のように天から落ちる
高い高い木の歌
針のような松の葉の香り
雨のあとの赤土の匂い
長い赤い首の歌
顔は真っ赤な罌粟の花色

66

大きな褐色の腕の歌
野原に咲いたデイジー　眼（まなこ）
ブラックとホワイトの　ブラックホワイトの　ブラックのひとたちの
白い手の歌も入れたいな
黒い手　褐色　黄色い手
赤い粘土の大地の手
やさしい指でみんなに触れる
いとも自然に互いに触れ合う
露のようにね
その暁の曲の中でね
もしも私が作曲家になれたなら
書くんだ
アラバマの夜明けの
その曲を

渡る

孤独な日だった　仲間よ
私は　ひとりで歩いていた
友達は私をぐるりと囲んでいたけれど
いなくなったみたいだった
私は山に登った
高所の　寒い風
私が着ていたコートは
蚊取網のように薄かった
私は谷に下りて行った
私は冷たい河を渡った
渡っている河の水は

夢の中の水ではなかった
私が履いていた靴は　冷たい河水から
足を護ってくれなかった
向こう岸で　私は草原に立った
見る限り
誰も草原にはいなかった
孤独な日だった　仲間よ
私は　すべて　ひとりで歩いた
友達は一緒にいたけれど
いなくなったみたいだった

島

悲しみの波は
もう　私を溺れさせない

私は　島を見る
いまだとにかく　前方に

私は　島を見る
砂は　輝いている

悲しみの波よ
私をそこへ　連れて行け

Ⅲ

夢屑

夢

夢をしっかりつかんでいろ
夢が死んだら
人生は羽を砕かれた鳥だ
飛ぶことが出来ない

夢をしっかりつかんでいろ
夢が去ったら
人生は不毛の畑だ
雪で凍り果てる

夢屑

集めよ　星屑から
　　大地の塵
霞の欠片（かけら）　雲の塵
手に一杯の夢の屑
　　売りません

アフロ系は河について話します

私は河を知っている
私は河を知っている　世界と同じくらい年輪を重ね　人間の静脈を流れる血
液よりも古い河を

私のたましいは深くなった　河のように

私はユーフラテス河に浸った　夜は明けたばかりだった
私はコンゴ河のそばに小屋を建てた　河は子守歌となり　私を眠らせた
私はナイル河を見下ろした　私はピラミッドを立ち上げた　その上に
私はミシシッピ河の歌を聞いた　エイブ・リンカーンが
ニューオーリンズにやって来た時

その泥だらけの胸は　夕陽に照らされ　すべて金色に輝いた

私は河を知っている
古代からの　ほの暗い河を

私のたましいは深くなった　河のように

アンニュイ

大いに
退屈だ
いつも
金がない

自殺したいよ

静かなる　河
冷たい　その顔
キスしろと

みじめブルース

ブルースを聞かせて
ブルースを聞かせて
私のみじめさを癒してくれるのは
ブルースだけなの

慰めの歌を歌ってください
慰めの歌と言ったのよ
私が愛していた男が　悪いことを
悪いことを私にしでかした

わからないの？

わかってください
善良な女が泣いている
悪い男のために

アフロ系の女には
私のような女には
ブルースが聞きたい
みじめさを癒すために

人生は素敵だ

河へ下って行った
岸に座った
考えようとしたけど　出来なかった
それで　河に飛び込んで　沈んだ

一度　浮き上がって　叫んだ
二度　浮き上がり　助けを呼んだ
河の水が　あんなに冷たくなかったら
沈んで　死んでしまっただろう

だけど　水は冷たかった　ひどく冷たかった

エレベーターに乗った
地上から十六階まで
つれない　僕の恋人
飛び降りようと思った

飛び降りて　死んじまっただろう
そんなに高くなかったら
そこに立って　助けを呼んだ
僕は立って　叫んだ

だけど　ひどく高いところ　高かった

それで　まだ生きている　ここで
生き続けるよ　僕は

81

君がつれないから　死にたかった
でも生きるために　僕は生まれてしまった

君　もし僕の叫びを聞いても
僕が助けを呼ぶのを見ても
僕はドジる　ねえ　可愛い君
僕が死ぬのを見てくれるなら

人生は素敵だ！　素敵だ！　人生は素敵だ！

縁切り状

きみ　どうして会ってくれないの？
僕　君の支払いは　ちゃんと払ってるんだ
毎週　週ごと

もし　誰かほかの男が出来たなら
言ってくれ——
でなきゃ　僕　君と縁を切る
君の家賃は払わないよ
いいかい
一文も

アフリカ

眠れる巨人
君はしばらく　休んでいたんだ

今　私は見る　雷鳴を
稲光を
君の微笑みの中に
今　私は見る
嵐の雲を
君の目覚めのまなこの中に
雷鳴
驚異

驚きの
若さ

君の歩みは　すべて
新たなる　大股闊歩
君の　太腿で

捕まえた

力持ちの男の子がやって来た
人魚を運ぶ
肩に担いで
人魚は　尻尾を
曲げていた
彼の腕の下

漁師の少年だから
見つけたかったのは　一匹のおさかな
運ぶためには――
半分魚

半分乙女（ハーフ）

結婚するためには

アフロ系の母

子どもたち　私が今日　戻って来たのは
お話するためです　長い暗い道について
私は上らなければならなかった
知らなければならなかった
私たち人種が生き　成長するために
私の顔を見なさい――夜のように暗い――
でも太陽のように輝いています　愛の真実の光で
私は　砂浜から彼らが盗んだ　その子供です
アフリカで　三百年前に
私は　そのアフロ系の少女です　広い海を渡りました
身体の中に潜む　自由の種を　運びました

私は　その女性です　畑で働きました

木綿とトウモロコシを収穫しました

私は　奴隷として働かされました

打たれ　殴られました　私の労働にもかかわらず──

子どもたちは　売られました　夫も売られました

安全も　愛も　尊敬も　私にはありませんでした

三百年　アメリカ南部の最も暗い地で

でも　神は歌を　祈りを　お与えになりました

今　子供たちのおかげで　私はかつての目標（ゴール）に近づいています

今　若くて　自由な　子供たちを見て

神の祝福は　私には拒否されていたのです　そう思います

私は　文字を読めませんでした　書けませんでした

夜の中へ戻って　私は　何も持ってはいませんでした

時々　谷は涙に満ちていました

でも　私は歩み続けました　孤独な年月でした

89

時々　道は　太陽の熱で熱かったのです
でも　私は歩き続けました　私の仕事が成就されるまで
私は　未来の　自由の種でした
私は　その夢を慈しみ続けました　私の胸の奥底で
誰も　それを押し潰すことはできません――アフロ系の母です
当時はそれは夢でしかありませんでした　でも今
あなたたちには　今日のアフロ系の者たちには
私の夢は　実現しているに違いありません
あなたたち世界中のダークの子供たち
忘れないでね　私の汗　私の痛み　私の絶望を
忘れないでね　悲しみで重かった　私の歳月を――
そして　悲しみのその歳月を　明日への松明にするのよ
私の過去を　光への道にするのよ
暗黒の中から　無知から　夜から　抜け出すのよ
塵の中から　私の旗を　高く　掲げてちょうだい

私の委託を支持して　自由な人間として立つのよ
権利を信じるのよ　誰もあなたを後退させない
忘れないでね　鞭で歩かされた　奴隷の道のりを
忘れないでね　強い者は　あらがい　闘ったことを
いまだ　道は　遮断されている　生きることは否定されている
見上げるのよ　いつも　太陽を　星たちを

私の子供たち　私は祈る　私の夢と祈りが
永遠に　あなたたちを　偉大な階段を上らせるように──
私はあなたと共にいる　白人の兄弟が誰も
アフロ系の母の子供たちを　卑下しなくなるまで

母から息子へ

息子よ　いいかい　私の言うことをお聞き
私には　人生は　水晶の階段ではなかった
鋲もあったし
ガラスの破片もあった
床板は　ぼろぼろで
ところどころ　カーペットは敷いていなかった――
裸の床だった
でも　やはり
私は上り続けた
踊り場まで上がり
隅っこを曲がり続けた

時々　暗闇の中へも進んだ
そこでは　光は　まるでなかった
だから　息子よ　引き返してはなりません
階段の上で　座り込んではいけない
なぜなら　わかって欲しい　苦難は　より親切な試練
落ちてはだめよ　今——
母はまだ　上り続けています　息子よ
まだ　上り続けています
人生は　水晶の階段ではありません

おはよう　とうさん

おはよう　とうさん！

私はここで生まれたんだ　そうおやじは言った

私は見た　ハーレムが大きくなるのを

アフロ系の人々が　拡がった

河から　河へと

ペン駅*1から

マンハッタンの真ん中を越えた

アメリカの人口の十分の一を占める

プエルトリコからの飛行便で

船を借り切って　若い者たちは

キューバ　ハイチ　ドミニカから

ニューヨークのマーク付バスで
ジョージア　フロリダ　ルイジアナから
ハーレムへ　ブルックリンへ　ブロンクスへ
でも　大部分は　ハーレムへ
マンハッタンのダークの帯[*2]
私は見た　アフロ系が　やってくるのを
驚きながら
目を見開いて
夢を見ながら
ペン駅から――
だが　列車は遅れた
門は開く――
でも　遮断棒がある
それぞれの門に

どうしたんだ　昔の夢を
まだ　見てるのかい？

とうさん　　聞こえるかい？

*1　ペン駅はペンシルバニア駅とも言われる。ニューヨークシティでは、グランドセントラル
　　駅と共に大きな駅である。
*2　ニューヨークシティはブルックリン、ブロンクス、マンハッタン、クィーンズ、スタテン
　　アイランドの五つの区から成り立っている。ハーレムと呼ばれる区域はマンハッタン区北
　　部に位置する。

96

カタツムリ

ちっちゃなカタツムリ
夢を見ながら　君は行く
天気とバラが
君知る　すべて

天気とバラが
君見る　すべて
飲んでいるのは
結ぶ露玉
その神秘

Ⅳ

霊歌

霊歌

岩と　不動の木の根
高く立ち上がる山々
強きもの　私の両手を置きます

歌え　主イエスよ！
歌は　強きもの
私は聞いた　母が歌うのを
傷つけられた　痛みの時

「私の馬車に乗って行くんだ　いつの日か！」

枝は立ち上がる
木の固い根っこから
山は立ち上がる
大地の固い膝から
波は立ち上がる
海の死んだ重さから

歌え　アフロ系の母！
歌は　強きもの

叫び

聞け　預言者の言葉を
幼子イエスよ！
聞け　聖者の言葉を！

イエスの足元

イエスの足元には
悲しみの　海
イエス様　あなたの慈悲が
漂い落ちて来ますように
私のところまで

イエスの足元に
あなたの足元に　私は立ちます
おお　幼子イエスよ
差し伸べてください　あなたの手を

祈り

あなたに伺います
どの道を行けばいいのですか？
あなたに伺います
どの罪を　耐えればいいのですか？
どの冠を　被ったらいいのですか？
私の髪の上に？
私は知りません
神様
私は知りません

祈り（2）

集まれ
あなたの哀れみの腕の中に
病める者　奪われた者
望みを失った者　疲れ果てた者
われらの倦んだ都市の
見捨てられた者たち
集まれ
あなたの哀れみの腕の中に
集まれ
あなたの愛の中に──
天なる神から　愛されてはいない
者たちよ

祈祷会

栄光あれ！　ハレルヤ！
夜明けは近づいた！
栄光あれ！　ハレルヤ！
夜明けは　やって来る！
アフロ系老女は小声で祈る
エベニーザー・バプテスト教会の*
最前席で
アフロ系老女は小声で祈る
夜明けは　やって来る！

106

＊
ジョージア州アトランタにある教会。アメリカンバプテスト教会派と連携。かつてマーチ
ン・ルーサー・キング師（父の方）と、同名の息子のマーチン・ルーサー・キング・ジュニ
ア牧師が一九六〇年から暗殺された一九六八年まで共同牧師を務めた。息子のマーティン・
ルーサー・キング（ジュニア）牧師は、一九五五年から暗殺された一九六八年までアフロ系
アメリカ人の公民権運動（Civil Rights Movement）のリーダーとして活動を組織、指導した。

黒いマリア

黒いマリアに違いない
私が見ているのは
黒いマリアを　私は見ている——
でも　私は願う
私のために　来ているのではないと

聞こえるかい？　二階で奏でられている音楽
私の心臓_{ハート}は
心配だらけ——
でも　二階で演奏の音楽は
私のためだ

君　太陽が
夜明けに昇るのを
見たことあるかい？
とっても面白いよ
ねえ　日の出を見たことがあるかい？
とっても面白いんだ　とっても面白いんだ
もしあるなら　君　そうなんだ　新しい一日が
始まったんだ

黒いマリアは通り過ぎる
昇った太陽を空に置き去りにして――
そうして　新しい一日が
そうだ　新しい一日が
始まった！

神

吾輩は神である——
ひとりの友すらなく
吾輩だけ　高潔を保つ
限りない世界の中で

下方で　若い恋人たちが
春の野原を歩んでいる
だが　吾輩は神である——
下りて行くわけにはいかない

春！

人生は　愛！
愛が　唯一の人生だ！
人間である方がいい
神よりも──しかも孤独な

十字架

かつて私の父は　ホワイトの老人
母は老いて　アフロ系
私が　ホワイトの老人を呪ったら
呪いを　引っ込めます

私がアフロ系の母を呪ったら
地獄にいろと願ったら
謝ります　悪かったと
今　母にはやすらかであれと願います

老いた男は死んだ　立派な大きな家で

母は死んだ　みすぼらしい小屋で
どこで私は死ぬのだろうか
ホワイトでもダークでもない私

皆でタンバリン

タンバリンを打て！
皆で　タンバリンを！
タンバリンを打て
神の栄光に！
タンバリンを打て
栄光のために！

ゴスペル[*1]は叫ぶ
ゴスペルの歌[*2]
人生は短い

でも　神は永遠！

タンバリンを打て！

皆で　タンバリンを！

タンバリンを打て

栄光のために！

*1　そもそもはイエス・キリストの説いた神の国と救いに関する福音。新約聖書の始めの四つの福音書の総称。

*2　黒人霊歌と黒人民俗音楽の要素が入った伝道用讃美歌。そもそもは十九世紀後半のアメリカのアフロ系の教会で歌われた聖歌に始まる。ゴスペルとも言われる。

映写

サヴォイ劇場が　改装されて[*1]

七番街まで跳んで

ハーレム・ルネッサンスと一緒に[*2]

ジルバを踊り出す　その日[*3]

アビシニア・バプテスト教会が[*4]

巨大な腕を伸ばし

聖ヤコブ長老派教会を抱き[*5]

409エッジコーム・アベニューが[*6]

身体をかがめて12西133通りにキスする[*7]

その日――

ほら！　イエスよ！

116

マンハッタン島は　ぐるぐる回り出すだろう

デイジー・ガレスビーのジャズを*8

イネズ・ティムが受け継ぎ　広めた*9

その日　主よ*10

サミー・ディビスとマリアン・アンダーソンは*11 *12

デュエットを歌い

ポール・ロブスンは*13

ジャッキー・メイブリーと*14

チームを組む

天なる神は　まさに　おっしゃるだろう

平和！
それは　本当に
素晴らしい！

＊1　サヴォイ劇場はブロードウェイの有名な劇場である。一九〇〇年に開設され、一九一〇年ごろからしばらく映画館として使用されたが、一九五二年に閉鎖。ヒューズが本詩を書いたこのころにはまだ現役の劇場であった。

＊2　ハーレム・ルネッサンスとはニューヨーク市マンハッタン区ハーレムで隆盛した、アフロ系の総合芸術運動。一九一九年から三〇年代の初期、あるいは中期まで及んだ。

＊3　ジルバとは英語jitterbugの日本語訛り。速いテンポでスイング（体を動かされるようなリズム感。ジャズの基本。一九三〇年代中期にベニー・グッドマン楽団が創始したと言われる）やリフトを行う社交ダンスとなった。チャールストンもそのひとつ。

＊4　アビシニア・バプテスト教会はハーレムの近隣、132ウエスト138番通りに位置するプロテスタントの教会。アビシニアとは旧エチオピア帝国の旧名。当時のアメリカ教会内での、アフロ系と白人の席分離への抗議を援助した。

＊5　聖ヤコブ長老派教会とはニューヨークのハーレム圏内にある、アメリカでは最も伝統のあるアフロ系アメリカ人のための長老派（新教）の教会。聖ヤコブの英語名はSt. Jamesであり、キリストの弟子十二使徒のひとり。

＊6　409エッジコーム・アベニューとはハーレム内にあり、W.E.B.など当時のアフロ系エリート・指導者が住んだアパート群が並んでいた。155通りのバス停からも近く、ハーレム・ルネサンス、のちにアフロ系公民権運動の拠点、会議の場所ともなった。アフロ系の人々が多く住んだシュガー・ヒル（145th-155th Street）の東端に位置する。

＊7　12西133番通りはハーレム内。ヒューズが一時住んだ場所。

＊8　デイジー・ガレスビー（一九一七─一九九三）。サウスカロライナ州出身。アフロ系アメリカ人の個性的なジャズ・ミュージシャン。トランペット奏者、バンドリーダー、作曲家。ビバップを普及。また曲がって上を向いたトランペット奏者でもあった。

＊9　イネズとはイネズ・カヴァナ。一九〇九年シカゴ生まれ。一九八八年？　カリフォルニア・ロングビーチで没。最初のアフロ系アメリカ人の歌手と言われている。ティム・ローゼンクランツと結婚。欧州ツアーを果たす。ヒューズの秘書でもあった。

＊10　ティム・ローゼンクランツ。一九一一年デンマーク生まれ。一九三四年に渡米。一九六九年ニューヨーク没。男爵の家柄。先祖はシェイクスピアの『ハムレット』に名が言及されている。ジャーナリスト、コンサートやレコードの制作に携わる。アフロ系歌手イネズと結婚。テレビ・ラジオの解説者、アナウンサー。ハーレム・ジャズの現場を伝えた最初のヨーロッパ系のジャーナリストである。

＊11　サミー・ディビス（ジュニア）。一九二五年ニューヨーク・ハーレム生まれ、一九九〇年カリフォルニアのビバリー・ヒルズ没。父はアフロ系アメリカ人、母はユダヤ系である。俳優でもあり、アメリカ最大のエンターテイナーとも言われる。

＊12　マリアン・アンダーソン。一八九七年フィラデルフィア生まれ、一九九三年アメリカ・ポートランド没。歌手として有名となった。アメリカばかりではなく欧州中でコンサートを開催。歌唱の幅も広く、ゴスペルから「アヴェ・マリア」、オペラ曲、クラシックなど多岐に及んだ。一九三九年、ワシントンD・C・のリンカーン記念堂で野外コンサート。一九六三年にはワシントン大行進でも歌った。他にも多くの栄誉に輝いているが、ホテル宿泊を拒否されるなど種々の人種偏見にもめげずに活動を続けたと記録は伝える。

13

ポール・ロブスン（一八九八―一九一六）。多言語で活躍したアフロ系アメリカ人。俳優、運動選手、黒人霊歌の歌手、バスバリトンのオペラ歌手、作家、公民権運動家。当時のソ連も含めてイギリス、ヨーロッパ、カナダなど各地で活動した。アフロ系アメリカ人へのリンチに反対して活動、黒人霊歌を演奏会場に持ち出した最初の歌手。ロンドンでミュージカル「ショーボート」、イギリスの映画監督ハニー・リチャードソン制作のシェイクスピア原作「オセロ」をストラット・フォードで演じ、次いでヨーロッパ、オーストラリア、ニュージーランドを回った。アメリカのラドガース大学、次いでコロンビア大学の法科大学院、ロンドン大学東洋アフリカ研究学院在学。父親はアフロ系の元奴隷であったが、自由を求めリンカーン大学を卒業した牧師であり、母は奴隷制廃止論者のクエーカー教徒の家族の一員であった。名家出身。ソ連への出入りにより一時アメリカ政府といさかいがあり、パスポートを剥奪されたりしたが、やがて返還された。

14

ジャッキー・メイブリー。一八九四年生まれ、一九七五年没。アフロ系アメリカ人のコメディアン、女優。デビューは、ニューヨークのハーレムにあるコニーズ・イン（地下のナイトクラブ）であったが、コニーズ・インはやがてダウンタウンに移り、ベシー・スミスやビリー・ホリディが出演した場所である。ジャッキーはアフロ系ボードヴィル（流行歌入りの軽喜劇、しばしば風刺を伴う）を得意とするコメディアンとして有名である。エド・サリバン・ショーなど、テレビ・ショーでも活躍した。

夢のブギ

おはよう　とうさん！
聞いたかい
ブギウギ大演奏？*1
遠い夢を　今話します

ビート　ビート──
彼らの拍子が聞こえるよ
じっと　聞いてよ

思わない？
浮き浮き　リズムって？

じっと　聞いてよ

聞こえない？

奥にあるもの

例えば――

　　何て言ったっけ？

もう　ラッキー！

私は　浮き浮き！

もちろん

　　ヘイ！　ポップ！

　　また　バップ！[*2]

モップ！

イェーーイ!

＊1 一九二〇代に黒人ピアニストによって創始されたジャズのリズムの一種。一小節八拍子のリズム基本に旋律が自由に演奏されるもの。やがてギターやベースなどの楽器に適用されるようになった。

＊2 一九四〇年代に始まったジャズの一種。あるいはバップダンスのパーティ。ビバップとも言う。

簡単ブギ

ベースの低音
乱れない　リズム
一歩　二歩　三歩
行進リズム

ベースの低音
いい気分　ドラムの連打
僕の好きな　僕の　リズム
僕の　ソウル

反復　連打　休止

ヘイ！　ねぇ　かあさん！

僕の言ったこと聞こえる？

簡単だよ　ブギダンス

ベッドの中で

リンチの影

暗い　月夜に
奴らは吊るした　アフロ系の男を
気を失うな
南部の淑女よ

見せしめに
暗い　月夜に
路傍の　木に
奴らは吊るした　アフロ系の男を

南部は見事さ　ホワイト女の

貞操の保護

南部の淑女よ
貞女であれ！
貞女であれ！

吊るされた少女の歌

場所は　南部　南部の州
（私の心臓は張り裂ける）
奴らは吊るした　私のアフロ系の恋人を
　　辻の木に

場所は　南部　南部の州
（傷だらけの死体が　宙づりに）
私は尋ねた　ホワイトの主イエスに
祈りはなぜに　役立たず？

場所は　南部　南部の州

128

（私の心臓は張り裂ける）

愛は　裸の影

こぶだらけの　裸の木の上

死にたいブルース

低音の　　眠たくなるような　弱拍の曲
前後に揺れて　　ベテランの歌声
私は聴いた　アフロ系アーティストの演奏
この間の夜　レノックス通りを下って
青ざめた顔のような　色褪せた　錆びた　古びたガス灯のそばで
彼は　ゆっくりと　体を揺すった……
彼は　ゆっくりと　体を揺すった……
ブルースの曲に合わせて
黒檀の両手を　象牙の鍵盤に乗せて
粗末なピアノに　メロディを呻かせた
おお　ブルース！

130

がたつく丸椅子の上で　体を前後に揺すりながら

彼は　悲しいが　へんてこな曲を演奏した　ミュージカルの道化役みたい

おお　ブルース！

アフロ系の人々の　嘆きの祈りから　生まれた

おお　ブルース！

深い歌声の中の　悲しみの調べ

私は聴いた　アフロ系の男の歌を　ピアノの呻きを──

「この世界に　仲間は誰もいない

俺は　たったひとり

やめよう　愚痴るのは

不満は　棚上げしよう」

ドスン　ドスン　ドスンと　彼は歩いて行った

少しギターを鳴らし　それからまた歌い出した──

「俺の歌は　死にたいブルース

131

俺は　この世に　満足できない
俺の歌は　死にたいブルース
この世は　不満だらけだよ──
しあわせなんか　とんでもないさ
いっそ　死んでしまいたい」

夜明け近くまで　彼は歌い続けた
星は消え　月も消えた
彼はやっと歌を止め　眠りに行った
ブルースは頭の中で　こだまし続けた
彼は岩のように眠った　あるいは　死んじまった男のように

＊

　ブルース（英語発音はブルーズ）とは、十九世紀後半、アメリカ南部でアフロ系アメリカ人の間で発祥し、やがて世界各地へ広まった音楽ジャンルである。アフロ系霊歌、教会で歌う聖歌、農作業の時の労働歌などから発展したと言われている。ジャズは楽器が中心であるが、ブルースはピアノやギターなどの伴奏を伴い、歌が中心である。ついでながら、ブルーとは憂鬱、気分が優れない、気分が落ち込んでいる、悲しい、嘆き、悲嘆などの意味合いがある。代表的な歌手の一人としてベシー・スミスの名前がある。

可哀想な少年ブルース

故郷にいた時
太陽は金色に　輝いた
故郷にいた時
太陽は金色に　輝いた
北部に来てから
世間は冷たくなった

悪いことはしていなかった
間違ったことはしなかった
そうだ　良い少年だった
間違ったことはしなかった
でも　この世はうんざりだ

134

面倒ばかりの　長い道

ひとりの少女（ギャル）に恋をした

親切だと　思ってた

少女（ギャル）に恋をした

親切だと　思ってた

僕から　銭　ふんだくった

気が狂いそうだった

死にたい　死にたい

死にたくなるよ　しらじら朝に

死にたい　死にたい

死にたくなるよ　しらじら朝に

人生　うんざり

生まれて来なきゃ　よかったに

ビリー・ホリディ*の歌を聞いて

忘れることは出来ない
その歌
その悲しさ
忘れることは出来ない
その悲しみの
歌だけは
忘れることは出来ない
その悲しみ
その歌
悲しみを語るな

塵で汚れた　彼女の髪　あるいは

目に塵が入ったまま

風がたまたま　吹き込んだ

私の　悲しみは

汚れる　絶望の塵で

弱音のトランペットの声

暖かい空気の中で　冷たい金管楽器

苦いテレビ画面は　ぼやける

揺らめく音で──

ここは　どこだ？

＊

　ビリー・ホリディは一九一五年生まれ、一九五九年ニューヨーク・ハーレムで没。アメリカ合衆国の代表的なジャズ女性歌手の一人。代表作に「奇妙な果実」がある。奇妙な果実とは木に吊り下げられたアフロ系の人々の死体のことである。（リンチ殺人）。作詞作曲はエイベル・ミューアボル（ペンネームはルイス・アレン。ユダヤ系）。彼は一九三〇年に新聞でアフロ系の男性死体二名の写真を見たと伝えられる。彼はまたルイス・アレンのペンネームで「苦い果実」という詩も発表している。「奇妙な果実」の方はビリー・ホリディが歌い、彼女は一九三九年からこの歌をレパートリーに加え、最後には必ず歌ったと伝えられる。

138

希望

時々　さみしくなるけれど、
どういうわけか？
この頃　ずっと考えている
だんだん
さみしくなくなるだろうと

ジュークボックス　ラブソング

ハーレムの夜を
きみに巻き付けよう
ネオンの光は　君の王冠
レノックス通りのバスの列
タクシー　地下鉄の喧騒
きみへの　ラブソング
ハーレムの心臓の鼓動を
ドラムで叩こう
そいつをレコードにして　ぐるぐる回し
ハートの音を　聞きながら
きみと　踊ろう　夜明けまで

きみと　踊ろう　きみはかわいい　褐色の娘に

解説

アメリカ文学の多様性の神髄がここにある

——ラングストン・ヒューズ英日選詩集『友愛・自由・夢屑・霊歌』（水崎野里子翻訳）

鈴木比佐雄

1

詩人で英文学者の水崎野里子氏から、昨年のアメリカ大統領選挙でアメリカ民主主義が根本的に問われている最中に、ラングストン・ヒューズの五十二篇の翻訳を読んで欲しいと言われた。新型コロナのパンデミックの進行により、黒人差別だけでなく、新型コロナの発生源とも言われる中国人への警戒が引き金となり、アジア系アメリカ人への差別は街角のヘイトクライム（憎悪犯罪）として、生々しい映像が飛び込んでくる。水崎氏は混迷する状況下で未来を照らし出すヒントがヒューズの詩の中にあると考えているようだった。

ヒューズの翻訳と言えば、詩人の木島始氏のことを思い浮かべるだろう。木島氏は私の出身大学の法政大学教授であり一九八〇年に小熊秀雄研究会を立ち上げ戦後間もない頃から翻訳されていた。木島氏のエッセイ集『郡鳥の木』によると、東大の卒論でフォーク

144

ナーの小説『八月の光』をテーマにしようと考え、指導教官の中野好夫氏に原書を借り
て読み、その中に出てきたハーレム・ルネサンスの黒人文学について興味を持った。た
ぶん中野氏の助言もあったのだろうが、ラングストン・ヒューズに心惹かれて、ついに
は私信を交わす関係にもなり翻訳を本格的に開始する。その翻訳がまとまった『ラング
ストン・ヒューズ詩集』は、書肆ユリイカ版、飯塚書店版を経て、一九六九年に思潮社
版として一一二篇を収録し刊行された。思潮社版は一九七〇年代初めまでは版を重ねて
いたが、現在ではほぼ絶版になっていて古本では入手出来ているようだ。私は小熊秀雄
研究会で交流した木島氏の影響でヒューズ詩集を読み、その翻訳詩や木島氏の解説に
よってヒューズは黒人文学という枠組みだけでなく、もっと根源的なアメリカ文学の本
質的な問題を提起している詩人であり、さらに言うならば人類的な観点を抱えて詩作を
している詩人だと、感じられていた。ヒューズが日本人に読まれるためには木島始氏の
先駆的な働きとそれを支援した出版社の活動も忘れてはならないだろう。

ヒューズの原文の詩集としては『The Collected Poems of Langston Hughes (Vintage
Classics ペーパーバック 1995/10/31 英語版 Langston Hughes(著), Arnold Rampersad
(編集)』があり、この中の膨大な詩篇群でも、選ばれた詩篇であり全詩集ではない。本書

は水崎氏がこの中から選りすぐり、今日的な情況の中で後世の人びとに読んでもらいたい五十二篇の原文の英詩とその翻訳の日本語版と英語版を合体させた編集になっている。

水崎氏は二〇〇七年にコールサック社が刊行した『原爆詩一八一人集』の英語版『Against Nuclear Weapons A Collection of Poems by 181 Poets 1945-2007』の翻訳者の一人となって頂いた。この日本語版・英語版は十数年経った今でも広島原爆資料館と長崎原爆資料館にて販売が続けられている。この英語版を読んだアメリカ人の核時代平和財団の創立者でありICANの設立にも関係することになるディヴィッド・クリーガー氏は、核兵器を廃絶するために原爆詩を書いて欲しいという英語版の呼びかけに呼応してくれて、コールサック社から『神の涙――広島・長崎原爆 国境を越えて/ God's Tears Reflections on the Atomic Bombs Dropped on Hiroshima and Nagasaki』を二〇一〇年に水崎氏の翻訳で刊行した。この『神の涙/ God's Tears』は一〇〇冊を刊行したが、その長崎原爆の被爆者から取材されて人類的な観点から書かれていることもあり、長崎原爆資料館ではロングセラーとなり初版が無くなり、十年後の昨年には増補版として二版目が刊行された。このように水崎氏は核兵器廃絶のための詩文学運動の翻訳活動で大きな貢献をしてきた。

また水崎氏は一九九九年『現代アメリカ黒人女性詩集』、二〇〇三年『現代アメリカアジア系詩集』、二〇一〇年『現代世界アジア詩集』（いずれも土曜美術社出版販売）などによって、従来の英米詩の系譜において顧みられなかったマイノリティの詩人たちのテーマや作品の魅力に注目し、その翻訳を長年続けてきた。詩論集としてもコールサック社で刊行した詩論集『多元文化の実践詩考』では、フランス、イギリス、アメリカなどの欧米の詩の歴史を見直して、多元文化という世界のマイノリティを視野に入れた観点から、世界の詩人たちの豊穣さを、翻訳を通して紹介している。

今回の水崎氏の翻訳は、ヒューズが一九六七年に亡くなってから半世紀以上経ち、またヒューズの翻訳詩集も絶版となりヒューズが忘れ去られている中で、ヒューズの詩篇の中にある普遍的な自由や人権の価値を問い、多くの人びとにその意味を問いかけたいという切実な思いがあるだろう。

2

木島始氏の『ヒューズ詩集』（思潮社版）は「大地の歌」「太鼓と十字架」「ブルースを演ってくれ」「ハーレムの呼び掛け」の四つに分かれているが、木島氏は特別な意味

はないと言ってどこからでもいいから読んで欲しいとあとがきで語っている。もし関心を持たれたならば原書を読んで欲しいとも付け加えている。本書は、水崎氏が高く評価する五十二篇の原文を左開きから収録し、ヒューズ詩の日本語の翻訳を右開きから収録した日英の合体版になっている。詩篇は「友愛」「自由」「夢屑」「霊歌」の四章に分けられていて、翻訳の文体も木島氏は「I」を「ぼく」、「僕」、「おれ」を使用して読者からの距離感を縮めて親密感を抱かせる文体である。水崎氏の文体では、「I」は「私」を中心にして訳し、時に内容によって「僕」を使用して自他の関係やその存在をクールに見つめるような視線が感じられる。ヒューズの代表的な詩「Let America Be America Again」の冒頭の原文と二人の翻訳を引用してみる。

《原文》

Let America be America Again.

Let it be the dream it used to be.

Let it be the pioneer on the plain

Seeking a home where he himself is free.

(America never was America to me.)

《アメリカを再びアメリカにしよう》 木島始訳

アメリカを再びアメリカにしよう。
今までありつづけた夢にしよう。
みずからを解放するホームを求める
かの曠野の先駆者にしよう。

（アメリカはこの僕にいちどもアメリカであったためしがない）

《アメリカを　再びアメリカに》 水崎野里子訳

アメリカよ　再びアメリカであれ
かつての　夢のアメリカに
かつて　草原の開拓者が　夢見たアメリカ

149

自由の国　アメリカに

（アメリカは私にはアメリカであったことはない）

　木島氏の訳はある意味で直訳的であり頭韻や脚韻の韻も原文に意味も忠実に移し替えようと試みている。三行目と四行目は入れ替えているがほぼ忠実に意味も訳されている。一行を空けて語られる括弧内の言葉では、木島氏の訳の「to me」はアフリカ系のアメリカ人の実存的な「僕に」である。

　一方の水崎氏の訳では、「アメリカ」が「夢」や「自由」そのものであり、その「夢」の「アメリカ」に立ち還るように「アメリカ」と「夢」をリズミカルに響かせていく意訳であり、韻も詩の意味を響かせる意味的な韻と言えるかもしれない。翻訳詩であるが詩としての完成度を重要視した作品を意識している。括弧内の「to me」はある意味でマイノリティの苦悩を抱え込みながらも、普遍的で共同主観的な「私には」を想定しているようだ。

　以上のような翻訳上の訳者の立場はどちらが優れているという問題ではなく、半世紀

150

以上前の翻訳と最も新しい翻訳を見比べた際の翻訳者たちの時代から求められる態度の違いであり、また現代のマイノリティを尊重するようになった現代社会の時代背景やその語感も大きな影響を与えるだろう。その意味では、水崎氏の訳を得たことによって、ヒューズはもっと深く日本社会に影響を与える可能性が出てきた。また原文もあるので英語の読める方ならば、英語が日本語になった場合に意味だけでなく韻律もどのように移し替えられて、芸術的な言葉になっていくかを想像して、バイリンガルを楽しむこともできる。

また水崎氏の翻訳された詩篇は、比較的にヒューズの思想・哲学・宗教観を理解できる詩篇群であり、「Ⅰ　友愛」では人類的な視点に立った自由、民主主義、友愛などの人類の理想とアメリカをリンクさせた崇高な長編詩だ。「Ⅱ　自由」では、自由を求めて夢の国に辿り着いた人びとが「アメリカ難民」になり、様々な差別や不条理に遭遇して苦悩していく試練をそのありのままを描いていく。「Ⅲ　夢屑」では、不当な扱いの中で心身も疲弊して存在の危機に至る精神状態になるが、アフリカ系の父母たちの底力やハーレムの「ブルース」の個人の底力によって、生きる力を甦らせてそれを乗り越えていこうとする。最後の「Ⅳ　霊歌」では、個人の内面の奥から湧き上がる「ブルー

151

ス」の囁きから発し、そのブルースが集まり多くの人びとの合唱のように、天上から神から降り注いでくる「霊歌（スピリチュアル）」と重なっていくかのようにヒューズは詠い上げていく。そのような思いで水崎氏は翻訳をされたように私は感じている。

葬り去るべき差別と不条理であるヘイトクライムが今も続くこの世界において、本来的な自由と人権と民主主義などに立ち還ることを促す「夢のアメリカ」をヒューズの詩篇から読んでもらいたいと願っている。この詩集は私たちの心のギフトになり、枯れることのない人類の文学的な財産となるに違いない。

詩人紹介

水崎野里子

ラングストン・ヒューズは一九〇二年、ミズーリ州ジョプリンで生まれた。高校在学中に詩・短編小説・脚本を書き始めた。一九二〇年（十八歳）に詩「アフロ系は河について話します」（The Negro Speaks of Rivers）が雑誌「危機」誌（Crisis）に掲載された。そしてニューヨークに本拠を置くコロンビア大学に一年間在籍。ハーレムに住んだ。時期はちょうど、アメリカ文学史上では「ハーレム・ルネッサンス」と現在では呼ばれている、一九二〇年代発祥のアメリカ・アフロ系の芸術・音楽（ジャズ、ブルース、黒人霊歌）・文学運動と重なり、その運動の文学部門を期待される、注目されるべき人材の一人となることになる。一九二五年に雑誌「機会」誌（Opportunity）の詩部門で最優秀賞を受賞した。受賞詩は「死にたいブルース」（原題は "The Weary Blues"）であり、翌年、一九二六年に出版の、ヒューズの第一詩集のタイトル・ポエム、すなわち詩集題名となった。旅行歴、放浪歴は生涯を通じて多い。船員として西アフリカ、ヨー

154

ロッパを訪れ、一時パリに住んだ。世界中の多数の国々に旅し、滞在した。後年ではソビエト連邦やハイチなど。講演では生涯にかけて全米を回っている。日本にも旅行している。

海外放浪から帰国後、まもなく詩によってヒューズは奨学金を授与され、ペンシルバニア州にあるリンカーン大学に入学し、一九二九年に学士号を獲得（卒業）した。リンカーン大学は、南北戦争（一八六一～六五）以前に既に別名で設立されていた大学である。そもそもは一八五四年に私立の教育機関として設立された。当時のアフロ系アメリカ人学生への隔離政策のためもあり、伝統的に、アフロ系アメリカ人学生を受け入れて来た教育機関であり、彼らに学位を与えた全米最初の大学である。一九七二年からは公的な教育機関となった。全寮制。アフロ系の弁護士、医師など多くを輩出している。また、一九六四年の公民権法施行（ジム・クロウ法＝人種隔離法の撤廃）以前に設立された、アフロ系アメリカ人のための公的な高等教育機関でもある。

一九四三年にヒューズは母校から名誉文学博士を授与されている。またグッゲンハイ

ム研究員助成金（一九三五）、ローゼンヴァルト研究員助成金（一九四〇）、アメリカ・アカデミー芸術文学奨励金（一九四七）を授与されている。一九二六年から彼の死の一九六七年まで、ヒューズは創作、講演旅行に貢献し続けた。彼は詩ばかりではなく、短編小説、自伝、歌詞、エッセイ、ユーモア作品、劇など、多彩なジャンルに渡って書き続けた。一九六七年、友人にも言わずに偽名で入院した病院で亡くなった。コミュニストとも言われ、その生涯は偏見と差別と闘い、ハーレムへの帰還、そしてアフロ系としての人権告発を続けた偉大な生涯であった。

ヒューズの詩は、かつてのアメリカ南部の奴隷制、リンカーンが奴隷制撤廃を掲げた南北戦争、一九二〇年代以降のハーレム・ルネサンス、一九五五年に始まったマーチン・ルーサー・キング・ジュニア牧師を主導者とする公民権運動、そして一九六四年の公民権法成立まで、アメリカの辿った苦難の道程の歴史の記録でもある。ヒューズは生きて公民権法（市民としての平等法）の成立を見た。また、民主主義はアメリカ建国の基礎であったはずであるし、神の下のすべての人間の平等は聖書に既に書かれている。ヒューズは絶えず解放を、自由を、平等を、友好を、我々に訴える。残念ながら、現在においても同じ状況、と付け加えよう。

（二〇二一年六月十八日記）

156

翻訳者解説　謝辞

ラングストン・ヒューズは生涯、彼の詩を理解する何人かの翻訳者や理解者・支援者に出会っているが、彼のあくなき差別への闘いと公正な人権への告発の底には、いつでも彼の、ゆるがない神への信仰があったような気がする。彼の作品全体をアフロ系霊歌・ゴスペル文学と名付けたい気がする。ひとつひとつ詩を訳して行ったが、いつも必ず宗教的な表現に出会った。

祈りとして、ヒューズは膨大な量の作品を書き続けた。孤独が、おそらくは神の沈黙へのいらだちではなく、むしろ神の言葉を具現しないアメリカ・世界への告発としてあった。マーティン・ルーサー・キング牧師の果敢な公民権運動の成就、ジム・クロウ法＝隔離法の撤廃を、ヒューズは死ぬ前に見たはずだ。本詩集は、それを見届けた男、一詩人に過ぎない者が経験した人生という苦難を歩んだ者から発せられた、夢と現実、希望と絶望の境を出入りして描いた、素直な神への告白である。彼は読者に神と、そし

て常に理想の人間を置いていた。彼の詩は、常にこの二人への語り掛けとしてある。こんなにさみしいものか、とは私の翻訳中の一貫した印象であった。さみしい男。

日本でもかつてアフロ系の詩や文学、そしてジャズなどは流行した。だが日本国内で日本語しか使用できない場合、日本人は単に「抵抗文学」のジャンルの中にこともなげにヒューズを入れてそれで終えてしまう傾向があったのではなかったか？ それも、海外文学のご研究の次元で、抵抗・差別告発文学と言えるなら言えるだけまだましである。かつても、またついこの間まで、否、いまだに、アメリカにおいては、人種差別・偏見反対と叫んだり抗議デモをしたり、一筆書いたりしただけでも、リンチ、すなわち虐殺の対象になった。（なる）。一方、最近ではアフロ系からアジア系への暴力、リンチ加害も見られる。（これにも、なんだ？ という感想はある）。

本著には木島始氏の前訳がある。だが本新訳は、コロナ（COVID-19）のパンデミックな感染状況をバックに二〇二〇年十一月末のアメリカ大統領選に至るまで高まった、前大統領トランプの言辞（かなり強硬な中国批判とコロナ感染政策の不備）と白人優位

の弁舌の中で、警察官とトランプの雷同者により相次いだ黒人リンチ事件に端を発する。

本著は本件への日本からの批判も込めて上梓された。コールサック社は早くはディヴィッド・クリーガーさんの原爆詩集『神の涙』（翻訳水崎野里子）を刊行した出版社であり、現在でもなおクリーガー氏の英語俳句を詩誌に掲載している。詩（ポエム）とペンによる（戦い）、告発（行動）の直接の交互作用を私に教えてくれたのは、アメリカ現代詩でもあった。それを日本で交互作用として受け止めてくれた出版社がコールサック社であった。コールサック社の関係者にこころより御礼を申し上げたい。

特に、いまだアメリカ文学の研究と翻訳がパイオニアであった時代に、ラングストン・ヒューズに出会い、愛し、翻訳した故木島始氏と、氏と個人的に交流を続け、かつての列島派につながる氏の文学と生涯を理解し、氏の精神を引き継いだ鈴木比佐雄氏に、繰り返し御礼を申し述べる。当時、英文学者の名の下でアメリカ現代詩を訳し始めた私のかつての不満も、木島氏も経験した、一九五〇年代以降のアメリカ現代詩全般の日本への受容と興味の手薄であり、英語文体の国際性への無理解でもあった。（曖昧さはむしろ許さない。はっきりと自分の意見を他者に向かって発言する。それがポエムと理解

されている）。

　他方、驚きがある。鈴木比佐雄氏は、いつのまにか日本では、「現代詩」との華々しい掛け声の下で消えて行った「列島派」の著作と文献を木島氏の死後もなお、大事に保持していた。英米文学者の目から見れば、たしかに、列島派は、一九五〇年代以降のアメリカ現代詩の歴史の直接の受容としてある。氏の文学者・編集者としての目の高さと、日本現代詩の未来的な展望と行方の探求の鋭さを評価する。その展望を日本の現代詩の中で受容する経緯での鈴木氏の孤独と苦闘と、氏のいつも独自で勇気あるエッセイと編集・出版業績に、心より謝辞を述べたい。

　なお、この翻訳本には、かつて私が上梓した『現代アメリカ黒人女性詩集』の延長でもある。当本の刊行に寄与していただいた故加藤幾恵さん（土曜美術社）に御礼を申し述べる。さらに、二〇一四年三月末に実施されたUPLI／WCP日本大会以降、親しくなった、アメリカ・カリフォルニアの詩人グループから誘われて二〇二〇年六月以降、今に至ってもなお英語単独使用で私が参加しているZOOM詩人会にも御礼申し上げる。主にコロナ感参加当初の彼らの詩の印象は、その暗さであり、暗さへの落下であった。主にコロナ感

染下の不安状況と、多大な犠牲を出したカリフォルニアの野火被害の詩が、暗さとして次々と発表されて行った。その中で、私は七夕など中国と共有する文化への言及詩から徐々に、しばしば芭蕉や蕪村の英訳付きで英語俳句や日本の豪雨被害の詩などを突っ込んで行くが、これは励ましていただいた。実は、ヒューズの詩に書かれているジャック・クロウ法はカリフォルニアではかつては日系人にも適用されたが、この経緯は彼らアメリカ詩人にも理解されているようであった。こちらの参加者のアメリカ現代詩人の方々にも感謝する。このカリフォルニアZOOM詩人会での私の参加聴講と詩の発表は、ほとんどこのヒューズの訳詩集の制作と重複していたことは明記する。

最後になるが、常に私を励ましてくださる詩人の皆様すべてに御礼を申し述べる。

二〇二一年夏

水崎野里子

石炭袋

ラングストン・ヒューズ 英日選詩集
友愛・自由・夢屑・霊歌
The Collected Poetry of Langston Hughes In English & Japanese
For Brotherly Love, Freedom, Dream Dust, and
Spirituals

2021 年 9 月 28 日初版発行
著　者　　　ラングストン・ヒューズ
翻訳者　　　水崎野里子
編集・発行者　鈴木比佐雄
発行所　株式会社 コールサック社
〒 173-0004　東京都板橋区板橋 2-63-4-209
電話 03-5944-3258　ＦＡＸ 03-5944-3238
suzuki@coal-sack.com　http://www.coal-sack.com
郵便振替　00180-4-741802
印刷管理　（株）コールサック社　制作部

装幀　松本菜央

落丁本・乱丁本はお取り替えいたします。
ISBN978-4-86435-490-5　C0098　￥2000E

Coal Sack Publishing Company
2-63-4-209 Itabashi Itabashi-ku Tokyo 173-0004 Japan
Tel: (03)5944-3258 / Fax: (03)5944-3238
suzuki@coal-sack.com　http://www.coal-sack.com
President: Hisao Suzuki

The Collected Poetry
Of Langston Hughes
In English & Japanese

For Brotherly Love, Freedom, Dream
Dust, and Spirituals

Translated by Noriko Mizusaki
COAL SACK PUBLISHING company

CONTENTS

I

Brotherly Love

Let America Be America Again

Let America be America again.
Let it be the dream it used to be.
Let it be the pioneer on the plain
Seeking a home where he himself is free.

(America never was America to me.)

Let America be the dream the dreamers dreamed —
Let it be that great strong land of love
Where never kings connive nor tyrants scheme
That any man be crushed by one above.

(It never was America to me.)

O, let my land be a land where Liberty
Is crowned with no false patriotic wreath,
But opportunity is real, and life is free,
Equality is in the air we breathe.

(There's never been equality for me,
Nor freedom in this "homeland of the free.")

Say, who are you that mumbles in the dark?
And who are you that draws your veil across the stars?

I am the poor white, fooled and pushed apart,
I am the Negro bearing slavery's scars.
I am the red man driven from the land,
I am the immigrant clutching the hope I seek —
And finding only the same old stupid plan
Of dog eat dog, of mighty crush the weak.

I am the young man, full of strength and hope,
Tangled in that ancient endless chain
Of profit, power, gain, of grab the land!
Of grab the gold! Of grab the ways of satisfying need!
Of work the men! Of take the pay!
Of owning everything for one's own greed!

I am the farmer, bondsman to the soil.
I am the worker sold to the machine.

I am the Negro, servant to you all.
I am the people, humble, hungry, mean —
Hungry yet today despite the dream.
Beaten yet today — O, Pioneers!
I am the man who never got ahead,
The poorest worker bartered through the years.

Yet I'm the one who dreamt our basic dream
In that Old World while still a serf of kings,
Who dreamt a dream so strong, so brave, so true,
That even yet its mighty daring sings
In every brick and stone, in every furrow turned
That's made America the land it has become.
O, I'm the man who sailed those early seas
In search of what I meant to be my home —
For I'm the one who left dark Ireland's shore,
And Poland's plain, and England's grassy lea,
And torn from Black Africa's strand I came
To build a "homeland of the free."

The free?

Who said the free? Not me?
Surely not me? The millions on relief today?
The millions shot down when we strike?
The millions who have nothing for our pay?
For all the dreams we've dreamed
And all the songs we've sung
And all the hopes we've held
And all the flags we've hung,
The millions who have nothing for our pay —
Except the dream that's almost dead today.

O, let America be America again —
The land that never has been yet —
And yet must be — the land where *every* man is free.
The land that's mine — the poor man's, Indian's, Negro's, ME —
Who made America,
Whose sweat and blood, whose faith and pain,
Whose hand at the foundry, whose plow in the rain,
Must bring back our mighty dream again.

Sure, call me any ugly name you choose —
The steel of freedom does not stain.

From those who live like leeches on the people's lives,
We must take back our land again,
America!

O, yes,
I say it plain,
America never was America to me,
And yet I swear this oath —
America will be!

Out of the rack and ruin of our gangster death,
The rape and rot of graft, and stealth, and lies,
We, the people, must redeem
The land, the mines, the plants, the rivers.
The mountains and the endless plain —
All, all the stretch of these great green states —
And make America again!

Freedom's Plow

When a man starts out with nothing,
When a man starts out with his hands
Empty, but clean,
When a man starts out to build a world,
He starts first with himself
And the faith that is in his heart —
The strength there,
The will there to build.

First in the heart is the dream.
Then the mind starts seeking a way.
His eyes look out on the world,
On the great wooded world,
On the rich soil of the world,
On the rivers of the world.

The eyes see there materials for building,
See the difficulties, too, and the obstacles.
The hand seeks tools to cut the wood,

To till the soil, and harness the power of the waters.
Then the hand seeks other hands to help,
A community of hands to help —
Thus the dream becomes not one man's dream alone,
But a community dream.
Not my dream alone, but *our* dream.
Not my world alone,
But *your world and my world,*
Belonging to all the hands who build.

A long time ago, but not too long ago,
Ships came from across the sea
Bringing Pilgrims and prayer-makers,
Adventurers and booty seekers,
Free men and indentured servants,
Slave men and slave masters, all new —
To a new world, America!

With billowing sails the galleons, came
Bringing men and dreams, women and dreams.
In little bands together,

Heart reaching out to heart,
Hand reaching out to hand,
They began to build our land.
Some were free hands
Seeking a greater freedom,
Some were indentured hands
Hoping to find their freedom,
Some were slave hands
Guarding in their hearts the seed of freedom.
But the word was there always:
    FREEDOM.

Down into the earth went the plow
In the free hands and the slave hands,
In indentured hands and adventurous hands,
Turning the rich soil went the plow in many hands
That planted and harvested the food that fed
And the cotton that clothed America.
Clang against the trees went the ax in many hands
That hewed and shaped the rooftops of America.
Splash into the rivers and the seas went the boat-hulls
That moved and transported America.

Crack went the whips that drove the horses
Across the plains of America.
Free hands and slave hands,
Indentured hands, adventurous hands,
White hands and black hands
Held the plow handles,
Ax handles, hammer handles,
Launched the boats and whipped the horses
That fed and housed and moved America.
Thus together through labor,
All these hands made America.
Labor! Out of labor came the villages
And the towns that grew to cities.
Labor! Out of labor came the rowboats
And the sailboats and the steamboats,
Came the wagons, stage coaches,
Out of labor came the factories,
Came the foundries, came the railroads,
Came the marts and markets, shops and stores,
Came the mighty products moulded, manufactured,
Sold in shops, piled in warehouses,
Shipped the wide world over:

Out of labor — white hands and black hands —
Came the dream, the strength, the will,
And the way to build America.
Now it is Me here, and You there.
Now it's Manhattan, Chicago,
Seattle, New Orleans,
Boston and El Paso —
Now it is the U.S.A.

A long time ago, but not too long ago, a man said:

> ALL MEN ARE CREATED EQUAL...
> ENDOWED BY THEIR CREATOR
> WITH CERTAIN INALIENABLE
>   RIGHTS...
> AMONG THESE LIFE, LIBERTY
> AND THE PURSUIT OF HAPPINESS.

His name was Jefferson. There were slaves then,
But in their hearts the slaves believed him, too,
And silently took for granted
That what he said was also meant for them.

It was a long time ago,
But not so long ago at that, Lincoln said:

> NO MAN IS GOOD ENOUGH
> TO GOVERN ANOTHER MAN
> WITHOUT THAT OTHER'S CONSENT.

There were slaves then, too,
But in their hearts the slaves knew
What he said must be meant for every human being —
Else it had no meaning for anyone.
Then a man said:

> BETTER TO DIE FREE,
> THAN TO LIVE SLAVES.

He was a colored man who had been a slave
But had run away to freedom.
And the slaves knew
What Frederick Douglass said was true.
With John Brown at Harpers Ferry, Negroes died.
John Brown was hung.

Before the Civil War, days were dark,
And nobody knew for sure
When freedom would triumph.
"Or if it would," thought some.

But others knew it had to triumph.
In those dark days of slavery,
Guarding in their hearts the seed of freedom,
The slaves made up a song:

  KEEP YOUR HAND ON THE PLOW!
   HOLD ON!

That song meant just what it said: *Hold on!*
Freedom will come!

  KEEP YOUR HAND ON THE PLOW!
   HOLD ON!

Out of war, it came, bloody and terrible!
But it came!
Some there were, as always,

Who doubted that the war would end right,
That the slaves would be free,
Or that the union would stand.
But now we know how it all came out.
Out of the darkest days for a people and a nation,
We know now how it came out.
There was light when the battle clouds rolled away.
There was a great wooded land,
And men united as a nation.

America is a dream.
The poet says it was promises.
The people say it *is* promises — that will come true.
The people do not always say things out loud,
Nor write them down on paper.
The people often hold
Great thoughts in their deepest hearts
And sometimes only blunderingly express them,
Haltingly and stumbling say them,
And faultily put them into practice.
The people do not always understand each other.
But there is, somewhere there,

Always the *trying* to understand,

And the *trying* to say,

"You are a man. Together we are building our land."

America!

Land created in common,

Dream nourished in common,

Keep your hand on the plow! Hold on!

If the house is not yet finished,

Don't be discouraged, builder!

If the fight is not yet won,

Don't be weary, soldier!

The plan and the pattern is here,

Woven from the beginning

Into the warp and woof of America:

ALL MEN ARE CREATED EQUAL.

NO MAN IS GOOD ENOUGH

TO GOVERN ANOTHER MAN WITHOUT

THAT OTHER'S CONSENT.

BETTER DIE FREE,

THAN LIVE SLAVES.

Who said those things? Americans!
Who owns those words? America!
Who is America? You, me!
We are America!
To the enemy who would conquer us from without,
We say, NO!
To the enemy who would divide
and conquer us from within,
We say, NO!

    FREEDOM!
        BROTHERHOOD!
            DEMOCRACY!

To all the enemies of these great words:
We say, NO!

A long time ago,
An enslaved people heading toward freedom
Made up a song:

Keep Your Hand On The Plow! Hold On!

That plow plowed a new furrow

Across the field of history.

Into that furrow the freedom seed was dropped.

From that seed a tree grew, is growing, will ever grow.

That tree is for everybody,

For all America, for all the world.

May its branches spread and its shelter grow

Until all races and all peoples know its shade.

KEEP YOUR HAND ON THE PLOW!

HOLD ON!

Brotherly Love

A Little Letter to the White Citizens of the South

In line of what my folks say in Montgomery,
In line of what they're teaching about love,
When I reach out my hand, will *you* take it
Or cut it off and leave a nub above?

If I found it in my heart to love you,
And if I thought I really could,
If I said, "Brother, I forgive you,"
I wonder, would it do *you* any good?

So long, so *long* a time you've been calling
Me *all* kinds of names, pushing me down —
I been swimming with my head deep under water,
And you wished I would stay under till I drown.

But I didn't! I'm still swimming! Now you're mad
Because I won't ride in the back end of your bus.
When I answer, "Anyhow, I'm gonna love you,"

Still and yet *you* want to make a fuss.

Now listen, white folks!
In line with Reverend King down in Montgomery —
Also because the Bible says I must —
I'm gonna love you — *yes, I will! Or BUST!*

> *Dr. King and Langston Hughes maintained a friendship for years. Hughes wrote this poem in 1956 during the 13-month Montgomery bus boycott.

Democracy

Democracy will not come
Today, this year
    Nor ever
Through compromise and fear.

I have as much right
As the other fellow has
    To stand
On my two feet
And own land.

I tire so of hearing people say,
Let things take their course.
Tomorrow is another day.
I do not need freedom when I'm dead.
I cannot live on tomorrow's bread.
    Freedom
    Is a strong seed
    Planted

In a great need.
I live here, too.
I want my freedom
Just as you.

II

Freedom

Refugee in America

There are words like *Freedom*
Sweet and wonderful to say.
On my heartstrings freedom sings
All day everyday.

There are words like *Liberty*
That almost make me cry.
If you had known what I knew
You would know why.

Georgia Dusk

Sometimes there's a wind in the Georgia dusk
That cries and cries and cries
Its lonely pity through the Georgia dusk
Veiling what the darkness hides.

Sometimes there's blood in the Georgia dusk,
Left by a streak of sun,
A crimson trickle in the Georgia dusk.
Whose blood? ... Everyone's.

Sometimes a wind in the Georgia dusk
Scatters hate like seed
To sprout its bitter barriers
Where the sunsets bleed.

Harlem

What happens to a dream deferred?

    Does it dry up
    like a raisin in the sun?
    Or fester like a sore —
    And then run?
    Does it stink like rotten meat?
    Or crust and sugar over —
    like a syrupy sweet?

    Maybe it just sags
    like a heavy load.

    Or does it explode?

New Yorkers

I was born here,
that's no lie, he said,
right here beneath God's sky.

I wasn't born here, she said,
I come — and why?
Where I come from
folks work hard
all their lives
until they die
and never own no parts
of earth nor sky
So I come up here.
Now what've I got?
    You!

She lifted up her lips
in the dark:
The same old spark!

Stars

O, sweep of stars over Harlem streets,
O, little breath of oblivion that is night.
    A city building
    To a mother's song.
    A city dreaming
    To a lullaby.
Reach up your hand, dark boy, and take a star.
Out of the little breath of oblivion
    That is night,
    Take just
    One star.

Lunch in a Jim Crow* Car

Get out the lunch-box of your dreams
And bite into the sandwich of your heart,
And ride the Jim Crow car until it screams
And, like an atom bomb-bursts apart.

*Once, in some states in the South, there were segregations in the
cars of a train, toilets, lanes, and others, in public, between white
people and colored ones. These regulations were called, as "Jim
Crow Laws."

One-Way Ticket

I pick up my life
And take it with me
And I put it down in
Chicago, Detroit,
Buffalo, Scranton,
Any place that is
North and East —
And not Dixie.

I pick up my life
And take it on the train
To Los Angeles, Bakersfield,
Seattle, Oakland, Salt Lake,
Any place that is
North and West —
And not South.

I am fed up
With Jim Crow laws,

People who are cruel
And afraid,
Who lynch and run,
Who are scared of me
And me of them.

I pick up my life
And take it away
On a one-way ticket —
Gone up North,
Gone out West,
Gone!

Freedom Train

I read in the papers about the
Freedom Train.
I heard on the radio about the
Freedom Train.
I seen folks talkin' about the
Freedom Train.
Lord, I been a-waitin' for the
Freedom Train!

Down South in Dixie only train I see's
Got a Jim Crow car set aside for me.
I hope there ain't no Jim Crow on the Freedom Train,
No back door entrance to the Freedom Train,
No signs FOR COLORED on the Freedom Train,
No WHITE FOLKS ONLY on the Freedom Train.

I'm gonna check up on this
Freedom Train.

Who's the engineer on the Freedom Train?
Can a coal black man drive the Freedom Train?
Or am I still a porter on the Freedom Train?
Is there ballot boxes on the Freedom Train?
When it stops in Mississippi will it be made plain
Everybody's got a right to board the Freedom Train?

> Somebody tell me about this
> > Freedom Train!

The Birmingham station's marked COLORED and WHITE.
The white folks go left, the colored go right —
They even got a segregated lane.
Is that the way to get aboard the Freedom Train?

> I got to know about this
> > Freedom Train!

If my children ask me, *Daddy, please explain*
Why there's Jim Crow stations for the Freedom Train?
What shall I tell my children? . . . *You* tell me —
'Cause freedom ain't freedom when a man ain't free.

But maybe they explains it on the
      Freedom Train.

When my grandmother in Atlanta, 83 and black,
Gets in line to see the Freedom,
Will some white man yell, *Get back!*
A Negro's got no business on the Freedom Track!

      Mister, I thought it were the
        Freedom Train!

Her grandson's name was Jimmy. He died at Anzio.
He died for real. It warn't no show.
The freedom that they carryin' on this Freedom Train,
Is it for real — or just a show again?

      Jimmy wants to know about the
        Freedom Train.

Will *his* Freedom Train come zoomin' down the track
Gleamin' in the sunlight for white and black?

Not stoppin' at no stations marked COLORED nor WHITE,
Just stoppin' in the fields in the broad daylight,
Stoppin' in the country in the wide-open air
Where there never was no Jim Crow signs nowhere,

No Welcomin' Committees, nor politicians of note,
No Mayors and such for which colored can't vote,
And nary a sign of a color line —
For the Freedom Train will be yours and mine!

Then maybe from their graves in Anzio
The G.I.'s who fought will say, *We wanted it so!*
Black men and white will say, *Ain't it fine?*
At home they got a train that's yours and mine!

Then I'll shout, *Glory for the*
    Freedom Train!
I'll holler, *Blow your whistle,*
    Freedom Train!
Thank God-A-Mighty! Here's the
    Freedom Train!
Get on board our Freedom Train!

Sailor

He sat upon the rolling deck
Half a world away from home,
And smoked a Capstan cigarette
And watched the blue waves tipped with foam.

He had a mermaid on his arm,
An anchor on his breast,
And tattooed on his back he had
A blue bird in a nest.

Lincoln Theatre

The head of Lincoln looks down from the wall
While movies echo dramas on the screen.
The head of Lincoln is serenely tall
Above a crowd of black folk, humble, mean.
The movies end. The lights flash gaily on.
The band down in the pit bursts into jazz.
The crowd applauds a plump brown-skin bleached
    blonde
Who sings the troubles every woman has.
She snaps her fingers, slowly shakes her hips,
And cries, all careless-like from reddened lips!
De man I loves has
Gone and done me wrong . . .
While girls who wash rich white folks clothes by day
And sleek-haired boys who deal in love for pay
Press hands together, laughing at her song.

I, Too

I, too, sing America.

I am the darker brother.
They send me to eat in the kitchen
When company comes,
But I laugh,
And eat well,
And grow strong.

Tomorrow,
I'll be at the table
When company comes.
Nobody'll dare
Say to me,
"Eat in the kitchen,"
Then.

Besides,
They'll see how beautiful I am

And be ashamed —

I, too, am America.

Daybreak in Alabama

When I get to be a composer
I'm gonna write me some music about
Daybreak in Alabama
And I'm gonna put the purtiest songs in it
Rising out of the ground like a swamp mist
And falling out of heaven like soft dew.
I'm gonna put some tall and tall trees in it
And the scent of pine needles
And the smell of red clay after rain
And long red necks
And poppy colored faces
And big brown arms
And the field daisy eyes
Of black and white black white black people
And I'm gonna put white hands
And black hands and brown and yellow hands
And red clay earth hands in it
Touching everybody with kind fingers
And touching each other natural as dew

In that dawn of music when I
Get to be a composer
And write about daybreak
In Alabama.

Crossing

It was that lonely day, folks,
When I walked all by myself.
My friends was all around me
But it was as if they'd left.
I went up on a mountain
In a high cold wind
And the coat that I was wearing
Was mosquito-netting thin.
I went down in the valley
And I crossed an icy stream
And the water I was crossing
Was no water in a dream
And the shoes I was wearing
No protection for that stream.
Then I stood out on a prairie
And as far as I could see
Wasn't nobody on that prairie
Looked like me.
It was that lonely day, folks,

I walked all by myself:
My friends was right there with me
But was just as if they'd left.

Island

Wave of sorrow,
Do not drown me now:

I see the island
Still ahead somehow.

I see the island
And its sands are fair:

Wave of sorrow,
Take me there.

Ⅲ

Dream Dust

Dreams

Hold fast to dreams
For if dreams die
Life is a broken-winged bird
That cannot fly.

Hold fast to dreams
For when dreams go
Life is a barren field
Frozen with snow.

Dream Dust

Gather out of star-dust
    Earth-dust,
    Cloud-dust,
    Storm-dust,
And splinters of hail,
One handful of dream-dust
    Not for sale.

The Negro Speaks of Rivers

I've known rivers:
I've known rivers ancient as the world and older than the
    flow of human blood in human veins.

My soul has grown deep like the rivers.

I bathed in the Euphrates when dawns were young.
I built my hut near the Congo and it lulled me to sleep.
I looked upon the Nile and raised the pyramids above it.
I heard the singing of the Mississippi when Abe Lincoln
    went down to New Orleans, and I've seen its muddy
    bosom turn all golden in the sunset.

I've known rivers:
Ancient, dusky rivers.

My soul has grown deep like the rivers.

Ennui

It's such a
Bore
Being always
Poor.

Suicide's Note

The calm,
Cool face of the river
Asked me for a kiss.

Misery

Play the blues for me.
Play the blues for me.
No other music
'LI ease my misery.

Sing a soothin' song.
Said a soothin' song,
Cause the man I love's done
Done me wrong.

Can't you understand,
O, understand
A good woman's cryin'
For a no-good man?

Black gal like me,
Black gal like me
'S got to hear a blues
For her misery.

Life Is Fine

I went down to the river,
I set down on the bank.
I tried to think but couldn't,
So I jumped in and sank.

I came up once and hollered!
I came up twice and cried!
If that water hadn't a-been so cold
I might've sunk and died.

>   *But it was*
>   *Cold in that water!*
>   *It was cold!*

I took the elevator
Sixteen floors above the ground.
I thought about my baby
And thought I would jump down.

I stood there and I hollered!
I stood there and I cried!
If it hadn't a-been so high
I might've jumped and died,

> *But it was*
> *High up there!*
> *It was high!*

So since I'm still here livin',
I guess I will live on.
I could've died for love —
But for livin' I was born.

Though you may hear me holler,
And you may see me cry —
I'll be dogged, sweet baby,
If you gonna see me die.

> *Life is fine!*
> *Fine as wine!*
> *Life is fine!*

Ultimatum

Baby, how come you can't see me
when I'm paying your bills
each and every week?

If you got somebody else,
tell me —
else I'll cut you off
without your rent.
I mean
without a cent.

Africa

Sleepy giant,
You've been resting awhile.

Now I see the thunder
And the lightning
In your smile.
Now I see
The storm clouds
In your waking eyes:
The thunder,
The wonder,
And the young
Surprise.

Your every step reveals
The new stride
In your thighs.

Catch

Big Boy came
Carrying a mermaid
On his shoulders
And the mermaid
Had her tail
Curved
Beneath his arm.

Being a fisher boy,
He'd found a fish
To carry —
Half fish,
Half girl
To marry.

The Negro Mother

Children, I come back today
To tell you a story of the long dark way
That I had to climb, that I had to know
In order that the race might live and grow.
Look at my face — dark as the night —
Yet shining like the sun with love's true light.
I am the child they stole from the sand
Three hundred years ago in Africa's land.
I am the dark girl who crossed the wide sea
Carrying in my body the seed of the free.
I am the woman who worked in the field
Bringing the cotton and the corn to yield.
I am the one who labored as a slave,
Beaten and mistreated for the work that I gave —
Children sold away from me, husband sold, too.
No safety, no love, no respect was I due.
Three hundred years in the deepest South:
But God put a song and a prayer in my mouth.
God put a dream like steel in my soul.

Now, through my children, I'm reaching the goal.
Now, through my children, young and free,
I realize the blessings denied to me.
I couldn't read then. I couldn't write.
I had nothing, back there in the night.
Sometimes, the valley was filled with tears,
But I kept trudging on through the lonely years.
Sometimes, the road was hot with sun,
But I had to keep on till my work was done:
I *had* to keep on! No stopping for me —
I was the seed of the coming Free.
I nourished the dream that nothing could smother
Deep in my breast — the Negro mother.
I had only hope then, but now through you,
Dark ones of today, my dreams must come true:
All you dark children in the world out there,
Remember my sweat, my pain, my despair.
Remember my years, heavy with sorrow —
And make of those years a torch for tomorrow.
Make of my past a road to the light
Out of the darkness, the ignorance, the night.
Lift high my banner out of the dust.

Stand like free men supporting my trust.

Believe in the right, let none push you back.

Remember the whip and the slaver's track.

Remember how the strong in struggle and strife

Still bar you the way, and deny you life —

But march ever forward, breaking down bars.

Look ever upward at the sun and the stars.

Oh, my dark children, may my dreams and my prayers

Impel you forever up the great stairs —

For I will be with you till no white brother

Dares keep down the children of the Negro mother.

Mother to Son

Well, son, I'll tell you:
Life for me ain't been no crystal stair.
It's had tacks in it,
And splinters,
And boards torn up,
And places with no carpet on the floor —
Bare.
But all the time
I'se been a-climbin' on,
And reachin' landin's,
And turnin' corners,
And sometimes goin' in the dark
Where there ain't been no light.
So boy, don't you turn back.
Don't you set down on the steps
'Cause you finds it's kinder hard.
Don't you fall now —
For I'se still goin', honey,
I'se still climbin',
And life for me ain't been no crystal stair.

Good Morning

Good morning, daddy!
I was born here, he said,
watched Harlem grow
until colored folks spread
from river to river
across the middle of Manhattan
out of Penn Station
dark tenth of a nation,
planes from Puerto Rico,
and holds of boats, chico,
up from Cuba Haiti Jamaica,
in buses marked New York
from Georgia Florida Louisiana
to Harlem Brooklyn the Bronx
but most of all to Harlem
dusky sash across Manhattan
I've seen them come dark
    wondering
    wide-eyed

       dreaming
out of Perm Station —
but the trains are late.
The gates open —
              Yet there're bars
              at each gate.

              What happens
              to a dream deferred?

       Daddy, ain't you heard?

Snail

Little snail,
Dreaming you go.
Weather and rose
Is all you know.

Weather and rose
Is all you see,
Drinking
The dewdrop's
Mystery.

IV

Spirituals

Spirituals

Rocks and the firm roots of trees.
The rising shafts of mountains.
Something strong to put my hands on.

    Sing, O Lord Jesus!
    Song is a strong thing.
    I heard my mother singing
    When life hurt her:

Gonna ride in my chariot some day!

    The branches rise
    From the firm roots of trees.
    The mountains rise
    From the solid lap of earth.
    The waves rise
    From the dead weight of sea.

Sing, O black mother!
Song is a strong thing.

Shout

Listen to yo' prophets,
    Little Jesus!
Listen to yo' saints!

Feet o' Jesus

At the feet o' Jesus,
Sorrow like a sea.
Lordy, let yo' mercy
Come driftin' down on me.

At the feet o' Jesus
At yo' feet I stand.
O, ma little Jesus,
Please reach out yo' hand.

Prayer

I ask you this:
Which way to go?
I ask you this:
Which sin to bear?
Which crown to put
Upon my hair?
I do not know,
Lord God,
I do not know.

Prayer [2]

Gather up
In the arms of your pity
The sick, the depraved,
The desperate, the tired,
All the scum
Of our weary city

Gather up
In the arms of your pity.
Gather up
In the arms of your love —
Those who expect
No love from above.

Prayer Meeting

Glory! Hallelujah!
The dawn's a-comin'!
Glory! Hallelujah!
The dawn's a-comin'!
A black old woman croons
In the amen-corner of the
Ebecaneezer Baptist Church.
A black old woman croons —
The dawn's a-comin'!

Black Maria

Must be the Black Maria
That I see,
The Black Maria that I see —
But I hope it
Ain't comin' for me.

Hear that music playin' upstairs?
Aw, my heart is
Full of cares —
But that music playin' upstairs
Is for me.

Babe, did you ever
See the sun
Rise at dawnin' full of fun?
Says, did you ever see the sun rise
Full of fun, full of fun?
Then you know a new day's
Done begun.

Black Maria passin' by
Leaves the sunrise in the sky —
And a new day,
Yes, a new day's
Done begun!

God

I am God —
Without one friend,
Alone in my purity
World without end.

Below me young lovers
Tread the sweet ground —
But I am God —
I cannot come down.

Spring!
Life is love!
Love is life only!
Better to be human
Than God — and lonely.

Cross

My old man's a white old man
And my old mother's black.
If ever I cursed my white old man
I take my curses back.

If ever I cursed my black old mother
And wished she were in hell,
I'm sorry for that evil wish
And now I wish her well.

My old man died in a fine big house.
My ma died in a shack
I wonder where I'm gonna die,
Being neither white nor black?

Tambourines

Tambourines!
Tambourines!
Tambourines
To the glory of God!
Tambourines
To glory!

A gospel shout
And a gospel song:
Life is short
But God is long!

Tambourines!
Tambourines!
Tambourines
To glory!

Projection

On the day when the Savoy
leaps clean over to Seventh Avenue
and starts jitterbugging
with the Renaissance,
on that day when Abyssinia Baptist Church
throws her enormous arms around
St. James Presbyterian
and 409 Edgecombe
stoops to kiss 12 West 133rd,
on that day —
Do, Jesus!
Manhattan Island will whirl
like a Dizzy Gillespie transcription
played by Inez and Timme.
On that day, Lord,
Sammy Davis and Marian Anderson
will sing a duet,
Paul Robeson
will team up with Jackie Mabley,

and Father Divine will say in truth,

Peace!
It's truly
wonderful!

Dream Boogie

Good morning, daddy!
Ain't you heard
The boogie-woogie rumble
Of a dream deferred?

Listen closely:
You'll hear their feet
Beating out and beating out a —

You think
It's a happy beat?

Listen to it closely:
Ain't you heard
something underneath
like a —

What did I say?

Sure,
I'm happy!
Take it away!

    Hey, pop!
    Re-bop!
    Mop!

    Y-e-a-h!

Easy Boogie

Down in the bass
That steady beat
Walking walking walking
Like marching feet.

Down in the bass
That easy roll,
Rolling like I like it
In my soul.

    Riffs, smears, breaks.

Hey, Lawdy, Mama!
Do you hear what I said?
Easy like I rock it
In my bed!

Silhouette

Southern gentle lady,
Do not swoon.
They've just hung a black man
In the dark of the moon.

They've hung a black man
To a roadside tree
In the dark of the moon
For the world to see
How Dixie protects
Its white womanhood.

Southern gentle lady,
 Be good!
 Be good!

Song for a Dark Girl

Way Down South in Dixie
    (Break the heart of me)
They hung my black young lover
    To a cross roads tree.

Way Down South in Dixie
    (Bruised body high in air)
I asked the white Lord Jesus
    What was the use of prayer.

Way Down South in Dixie
    (Break the heart of me)
Love is a naked shadow
    On a gnarled and naked tree.

The Weary Blues

Droning a drowsy syncopated tune,
Rocking back and forth to a mellow croon,
    I heard a Negro play.
Down on Lenox Avenue the other night
By the pale dull pallor of an old gas light
    He did a lazy sway....
    He did a lazy sway....
To the tune o' those Weary Blues.
With his ebony hands on each ivory key
He made that poor piano moan with melody.
    O Blues!
Swaying to and fro on his rickety stool
He played that sad raggy tune like a musical fool.
    Sweet Blues!
Coming from a black man's soul.
    O Blues!
In a deep song voice with a melancholy tone
I heard that Negro sing, that old piano moan —
    "Ain't got nobody in all this world,

            Ain't got nobody but ma self.

            I's gwine to quit ma frownin'

            And put ma troubles on the shelf."

Thump, thump, thump, went his foot on the floor.

He played a few chords then he sang some more —

            "I got the Weary Blues

            And I can't be satisfied.

            Got the Weary Blues

            And can't be satisfied —

            I ain't happy no mo'

            And I wish that I had died."

And far into the night he crooned that tune.

The stars went out and so did the moon.

The singer stopped playing and went to bed

While the Weary Blues echoed through his head.

He slept like a rock or a man that's dead.

Po' Boy Blues

When I was home de
Sunshine seemed like gold.
When I was home de
Sunshine seemed like gold.
Since I come up North de
Whole damn world's turned cold.

I was a good boy,
Never done no wrong.
Yes, I was a good boy,
Never done no wrong,
But this world is weary
An' de road is hard an' long.

I fell in love with
A gal I thought was kind.
Fell in love with
A gal I thought was kind.
She made me lose ma money

An' almost lose ma mind.

Weary, weary,
Weary early in de morn.
Weary, weary,
Early, early in de morn.
I's so weary
I wish I'd never been born.

Song for Billie Holiday

What can purge my heart
    Of the song
    And the sadness?
What can purge my heart
    But the song
    Of the sadness?
What can purge my heart
    Of the sadness
    Of the song?

Do not speak of sorrow
With dust in her hair,
Or bits of dust in eyes
A chance wind blows there.
The sorrow that I speak of
Is dusted with despair.

Voice of muted trumpet,
Cold brass in warm air.

Bitter television blurred
By sound that shimmers —
    Where?

Hope

Sometimes when I'm lonely,
Don't know why,
Keep thinkin' I won't be lonely
By and by.

Juke Box Love Song

I could take the Harlem night
and wrap around you,
Take the neon lights and make a crown,
Take the Lenox Avenue busses,
Taxis, subways,
And for your love song tone their rumble down.
Take Harlem's heartbeat,
Make a drumbeat,
Put it on a record, let it whirl,
And while we listen to it play,
Dance with you till day —
Dance with you, my sweet brown Harlem girl.

Hisao Suzuki
Here the American Spirit for Democracy, Equality and
Diversity
—— On the Collected Poetry of Langston Hughes in
English & in Japanese:
For Brotherly Love/ Freedom/ Dream Dust/ and
Spirituals
Translated by Noriko Mizusaki & Published by Coal
Sack Publishing Company

Last year, in 2020, while we were trying to think of the essential
questions on democracy, and while US had the election campaign for the next US President, I had a mail from Professor
Noriko Mizusaki, a poet and a translator, that she wanted me to
read the Japanese translations of the 52 poems by Langston
Hughes, which she translated. It was just at the time when the
COVID-19 was pandemic and infecting all over the world.
When we watched the news reports on TV, the real-time pic-
tures we had to watch one after another, not only the hate crimes
to the Afro-American people, but also the ones to the Asian-
American citizens. She might have thought that the poems of
Langston Hughes might have some hints, under the confusing
situation at that time, which would help us to light up our future.

As for the translations of the collected poetry of Langston

Hughes, we have to mention the previous translator, the late Hajime Kijima, who was a professor of Hosei University in Tokyo, as well as a poet, and who started reading the American literature including William Faulkner, which means he was one of the pioneers on the American Studies, at that time. He started translating Langston Hughes, as early as just after the end of the World War II.

According to Hajime Kijima, in the one of his essays, he thought of writing an essay on "Light in August" by William Faulkner, for his graduate thesis. He studied in the University of Tokyo. One day he borrowed the book in English, from his tutor, Professor Yoshio Nakano. Reading the book, "light in August," he was to be given a key led to the Afro-American literature and, especially, to Hughes and the Harlem Renaissance. Probably he would have had also some advice from Professor Nakano, I think. He started personal correspondences with Hughes and started translating his works, strongly being attracted by him.

"The Collected Poems of Langston Hughes" was first published in Japan, by Hajime Kijma, a professor, a poet and a translator. He first published it from Eureka Bookstore, then from Iizuka Publisher and lastly from Shichosha Publishing Company in 1969, which contained as many as 112 poems of Langston Hughes. The Shichosha version was repeatedly republished till

at the beginning of the 1970s, but turned out of stocks and at the present, only the recycled ones we can get.

In my personal case, it was a poet & the translator, Hajime Kijima himself, who influenced upon me to read the poems of Langston Hughes in his Japanese translations. At the time I stayed closer to Professor Kijima, because I was a student of Hosei University, and I was attending the gathering for reading Hideo Oguma, set up in 1980, There I frequently had occasions to speak with Hajime Kijima. I read also his essays or notes on Hughes. I think when we want Japanese readers to read more of the poems of Langston Hughes, we should not forget Hajime Kijima, who worked as a pioneer, as well as the supports of the publishing companies which published his books in Japan.

In the course of my reading the poems of Langston Hughes, I came to think that he was a poet, whose poems we should read not only in the genre of the just Afro-American literature, but also as a poet who dared to pose us fundamental and spiritual questions essential to the American literature. Besides, I even thought that he was a poet, holding rather a global point of view.

And further I would say that, Langston Hughes was working his mission, or writing his poems, holding a wider point view. It was just like the humanistic one. He covered all the humans and all

the people on the earth. On the other hand, in order that for Japanese readers to read more of his works in Japan, we should not forget the pioneer works of Hajime Kijima, as well as the supports of the publishers which published his books.

As for the English publications of the poetry of Langston Hughes, there is "The Collected Poems of Langston Hughes" (Vintage Classics) by Langston Hughes and edited by Arnold Rampersad and "Selected Poems" by Langston Hughes (1959/6/27). Though, he wrote a great number of poems in his life. So, neither of them contained all of his works. We edited and published the 52 poems that Professor Noriko Mizusaki chose and selected among from his works, considering on the political as well as the covid-19 situation we faced and are facing, in the present world. We wish all of us will read the book, in the present and in the future. The poetry book of the Coal Sack version was published in English & in Japanese, which means we combined English original poems by Hughes and the Japanese translations by Noriko Mizusaki, together, in one book, in a bilingual style.

Noriko Mizusaki worked with us as one of the translators of the anthology on Hiroshima & Nagasaki. The title is "Against Nuclear Weapons/A Collection of Poems by 181 Poets 1945-2007." It was published in the style of the bilingual anthologies,

in both the languages of English & Japanese, which have been still on sales and exhibited at the bookshops of the Hiroshima Peace Memorial Museum and the Nagasaki Atomic Bomb Museum. After the publication, Dr. David Krieger in US, who read the anthology, mailed to us one day, responding to our request to the poets for their writing poems on Hiroshima & Nagasaki. He mailed to us, that he was writing such poems. In the result he published his poetry book, "God's Tears/ Reflections on the Atomic Bombs Dropped on Hiroshima & Nagasaki," which was published also from the Coal Sack Publishing Company in 2010. Noriko Mizusaki took the part of the Japanese translations. Later, Dr. David Krieger also engaged himself in the organization of ICAN, as a president (at the time) of the Nuclear Age Peace Foundation and a poet. ICAN was awarded with the Nobel Prize for Peace, in 2017.

We published the book, "God's Tears" in the first edition, with one thousand copies, but it came to be out of stocks. So last year we edited the second version as the supplemental, partly because the first edition was reported by the hibakushas: by the victims of the Nagasaki A-Bomb explosion. Owing to them, the book could have added more humanistic points of views. In Nagasaki, they had been in long sellers. We thank for the professor, for her great dedication to the peace activity for the abolishment of nuclear weapons, through her translating work.

She published "The Contemporary Poetry of Afro-American Women" (1999), "The Contemporary Asian American Poetry" (2003), and "The Contemporary World Asiatic Poetry" (2010), in Japanese translations from the English originals, which means she had been taking special notices on the works and cultures of "the minority people" in the world. She would have been wishing to give them special spotlights, through her translating efforts. As for her essays, she published "The Collected Essays on Multiplicity of Cultures and Its Practice," from the Coal Sack Publishing Company (printed in Japanese). In the work, she introduced the diversities and the richness of the minority people. By the way, she included Japanese people and their cultures in the group.

In the Japanese modern history, especially in the postwar period of the World War II, Japan was strongly influenced by the West cultures, mainly from the winning countries; UK, France, and USA. While, some people started to say, that Japan started to lose her own identities, and skipped Asian countries and the minority people, outside and inside Japan. She posed us a renewed world map, which included the small, the ignored and the bullied people, using new terms like "the diversity" and "the multiplicity." In the result, she included the minorities' cultures and poems into the history of the world poetry, which is valued

as more international, today.

Her translation of Hughes poems is also included in her works
on the minority. She posed us her sincere and insistent love and
compassion again. She likely wants to ask the questions again
on the liberty and the human equality, for which Hughes also
had quested for throughout his life: also in Japan, partly because
the previous translator, Hajime Kijima's translating versions,
now almost go out of stocks. In addition, the poet himself,
Langston Hughes seems in the course of being forgotten.
Besides, it passed more than half a century, since he passed away.

I think the new translating version by Noriko Mizusaki, should
send you a kind of the wider perspective of the poet, Langston
Hughes. We can rather clearly understand his thoughts, his phi-
losophy, and his religious faiths. In the part I: "Brotherly Love,"
he showed us longer poems, linking America and his ideals,
such as liberty, democracy, and brotherly love. In the part II;
"Freedom," he depicted the people who came to America, seeking for liberty, and had to live as "the refugees of America," living
through various racial distinctions and hardships. In the part III:
"Dream Dust," he showed himself totally exhausted with the
injustices in his life, and sometimes driven into the mental crisis
but he was encouraged by the toughness of Afro-American people, with the mothers and fathers. He was also encouraged by

the blues, and regained the energy for life to overcome hardships. In the Part IV: "Spirituals," He sang his poems up to the heaven. Having had first started with blues, just like welling up from the depth of the heart of a singer, then, he moved into the spirituals, or gospels. They were sometimes sung in a chorus, by the people gathering together. They were sometimes lonely prayers by the poet. He was singing them alone up to the god in the heaven or with his friends together. At the same time, we can feel as if the songs were falling down from the heaven, or from the god.

Lastly I wish that all of us should all read his poems in this book. In this world, where hate crimes are still happening, violating civil rights, they shall certainly suggest us that we should return once more again, to freedom, to human rights (civil rights), and to democracy. These are original bases to us. So they should be. I believe that this book will certainly work as a healing light to our hearts, and that it will continue to be valued high as one of the eternal properties, to all of us, at any time and any place, in the world.

(English Translator: Noriko Mizusaki).

Profile of Langston Hughes (1902~1967)
By Noriko Mizusaki

Langston Hughes was born in 1902, in Joplin, Missouri. It was a town on the Mississippi River. In his high school days, he started writing poems, short novels, and plays. In 1920, when he was twenty years old, his poem, "My River" was published in the magazine, "The Crisis." Then he studied in Columbia University, in New York, for just a year, when he lived in Harlem.

At the present, the prosperity of the Afro-American poetry, arts and music in the 1920s, is called as "Harlem Renaissance." It was a movement for promotion and a propagation of the "black" arts and cultures.: gospel songs, jazz music, blues, etc. Hughes was supposed to be active as the member, in the movement. In 1925, he won the best prize with his poem, "The Weary Blues," which was to be a title poem of his poetry book, published the next year under the same title, in 1926.

He had so many travels or wanders. It is told that when he was young, he worked as a sailor and visited Africa, as well as Euro-countries. He lived in Paris. As a poet, later, he travelled to so many countries, including Russia and Haiti. For lectures, he traveled around all over in USA, for his life, invited. He also visited Japan.

Having returned home from his wanders in foreign countries,

he was awarded with scholarship through his poetry. He was admitted to Lincoln University in Pennsylvania, where he took the bachelor's degree. That is, he graduated from the university. Lincoln University was a historical university, which had been instituted before the Civil War (1861~1965). Originally, it was instituted as a private educational institute for the Afro-American students, because of the segregating policies between the black students and the white ones. Traditionally, Lincoln University had been admitting Afro-American students and it is the first university in USA, which awarded them with the academic degrees. In 1972, Lincoln University was turned into a kind of public educational institute. All the students have to live in the dormitory. Though, originally, it was a kind of public university for Afro-American students. The University has been sending out, so many human resources, as lawyers, medical doctors, poets and professors. It is now a public educational institute. We should take the notice that it had been instituted long before the enforcement of Civil Laws in 1964, in which, any differentiations or racial distinctions were declared and regulated to be unlawful.

In 1943 Hughes was awarded with an Honorary Doctor of Literature from Lincoln University. He also was awarded a Guggenheim Fellowship (1935), a fellowship from the Rosenwald Fund (1940) and Academy Award of the American

Academy of Arts and Letters (1947), etc. Since 1926 to 1967, when he passed away, he continued to dedicate himself to writings and lectures. Not only poems, he wrote short novels, autobiographies, words for songs, essays, works for humors, and plays, for life, in so many varieties. He passed away in 1967, alone, using a false name, in the hospital, without saying anything to his friends. His life was a great one, fighting against the prejudice and the segregation to the Afro-American people. For a poet, he did not stop writing for love, peace, and tender hearts, as well as for democracy, liberation, and human equality, which were originally the bases of the Declaration of independence of the USA. He also expressed out the Afro-American cultures and their daily lives. He always returned to Harlem in New York.

In the perspective of the American history, the African people were forced to be caught and shipped out to America, as slaves in the old time when America was in the colonies of Spain, UK and France. Then the North won in the Civil War, in which Lincoln held up the liberation of slaves, as a slogan. Then the Harlem Renaissance, which started in 1920s and the campaign of the liberation of the Afro-Americans, or the demonstrations for the Civil Rights, led by Rev. Martin Luther King (Jr), till the enforcement of the Civil Rights in 1964. The campaign had so many victims, including the leader, Rev. King, who was shot. In

the history, including the dark, originally democracy was the very spirit and the base for the foundation of the United States of America.

On the other hand, the Bible says everyone should be equal under the god. We should be all equal, even though it is still in the ideal. The poems of Langston Hughes covered all these backgrounds in the US history. He lived to see the Civil Rights realized, in 1964.

From Translator: Additional Notes on Langston Hughes
&
Acknowledgments
Noriko Mizusaki

Langston Hughes met and exchanged friendship with not a few supporters, fans and friends, who could understand his poems well, including translators in his life. At the base of his poems, there exist the most simple and constant prayers to the god, which was the consistent impression of mine, to the poet, Langston Hughes.I would feel like giving his whole works, the name of the Gospel literature, or the Gospel song. In the process of my translating, or my putting his each poem into Japanese language, I always met with some religious words or expressions. For his own prayers, he had been working out tremendous amounts of works and poems. How solitary a man he is, which was his impression to me, from the beginning to the end. I now understand that his solitary was not for the irritation to the god's silence, but for the accusation to the people in the world, who cannot understand humans are all equal and cannot know what the humanity is.

The US history in the 1960's experienced the brilliant achievements or the enforcement of civil rights, which late Reverend Martin Luther King (Junior) organized as the one of the leaders

and bravely fought against the racists. The Jack-Crow regulations were abolished, by the US President Kennedy and his successor, US President Lyndon Johnson. This poetry book of Hughes is also to be the witness. He prayed to the god, coming in and out between a dream and a reality, or between hope and despair, living through a hard life. His poems are conversations with the god and humans he loved. Though, how solitary was he, which was a constant impression to me.

One more comment, I'd add. In Japan, decades ago, Afro-American poets and their literary works and their music, called jazz, gained popularity and prospered and is now still prospering. But, in Japan, the Japanese poets tended only putting Hughes in the category of the resistance poetry or the protesting literature of the racial prejudice or for the civil rights, and having got satisfied, they soon forgot them, didn't they? It would have been better, even a bit, than having done nothing, or having no interests. Though, the one of the most important spirits in his poems is love, or tenderness to others. In USA, till just recently, when they shouted the oppositions at the racial discriminations or joining the demonstrations, or even writing it on even one line, some of them were shot down or lynched to death. On the other hand, just recently TV news showed us some Afro-American people in turns tried to beat or hurt some Asian American citizens on the streets. (It is a pity, too).

The Japanese translation of Langston Hughes had previous versions, by a Japanese poet and a translator, Hajime Kijima. He thought that the spirit of Langston Hughes poetry is love or tenderness, which I now here note down. He loved the works of Hughes and translated so many of them. He corresponded with the poet himself. He was also a reputed professor of the American literature, and almost a pioneer of the studies and the translation. He wrote children stories, too. Probably he might have lived Hughes, for his life. He might have also lived the hardship as a poet, in the Japanese poetical and cultural background in the period after the World War II. His preference of simplicity and tenderness seemed to have a bit of difficulty, together with the political aggressiveness to the majority. I send great thanks to Hajime Kijima.

This book started to be planned in the accidents that Afro-American people were started to be killed one after another. It was at the time under the administration of the former US President Donald Trump, whose speeches were sadly radical on the superiority of the white people for the great USA. He also delivered rather aggressive speeches against China, which had been in the prime around the time of the election of a new US President. Besides, it was during the time when the covid-19 was becoming more and more "pandemic," throughout the

world. Indeed, it was just a shot of American history, though, all the world lived with them and watched them. Where is gone, the brilliant American democracy? Once we wondered, with great puzzlements.

The Coal Sack Publishing Company once published the book, titled in "God's Tears," (the Japanese translation by Noriko Mizusaki), by Dr. David Krieger. In the English original version, brilliantly he declared peace, love, and equality, among humans. He is a consistent peace activist. In the book, he accused of A-bombs which were dropped on Hiroshima and Nagasaki, in 1945, just before the end of the World War II. And, they, the Coal Sack staff, are still publishing David's English haiku poems, in the original English with Japanese translations of mine, in the Coal Sack magazines.

Once, the US contemporary poetry taught us on the links between poems and political or historical activities. It was received and succeeded in Japan, mainly by the Coal Sack staff, in their own Japanese ways. They received it to extend, combining his work with the contemporary Japanese poetry, including Japanese haiku and tanka poems. The publication of this poetry book of Langston Hughes is on the same line: fighting for peace and love, international. This book, "the Collected Poetry of Langston Hughes," is published as a co-planning and

co-production between the Coal Sack Publishing Company and, a poet and translator, Noriko Mizusaki. I'd say, great thanks to the staff, too, and lastly, to Hughes himself.

Sincerely,
Wishing the world peace and love,
Noriko Mizusaki
In the end of May. 2021.
UPLI/ WCP Vice President
poet and translator

"The Collected Poetry of Langston Hughes
In English & Japanese
For Brotherly Love, Freedom, Dream Dust, and Spirituals"

Poems Quated From & Referred To

"Selected poems of Langston Hughes"
Vintage classics edition September 1990
Copyright 1959 by Langston Hughes

Noriko Mizusaki *Profile*

Born in Tokyo. Now Living in Chiba, Japan. She traveled to so many places in the world. She attended many poetry festivals international. She is a poet including tanka & haiku, a translator, and writing essays.

*Her Books of Translations from English to Japanese, with Essays: *"Poetry of UK & USA with Essays," "The Poetry and Essays For Pluralism & the Practices"* (Published from Coal Sack Publishing Company), *"For the Future of Poetry & Literature International" "On the Poetry International and the Essays" "On the Portrait of Family Members: in Ireland and in Japan"* (In Japanese)
*Her Books of Collected Poems Edited and Translated: *"The Contemporary Poetry of UK & USA" "The Contemporary American Poetry of Black Women" "The Contemporary Irish Poetry" "The Contemporary Asian Poetry of USA" "The Contemporary Asiatic Poetry International"* (In Japanese)
*Her Books Bilingual, for Peace: Published from Coal Sack Publishing Company: *"Against Nuclear Weapons: Collected Poems of 181 Poets"* (In English/ Joint Translation) The Book was Awarded with the 18th Peace Prize in Memorial of Kenji Miyazawa. David Krieger, *"God's Tears/ Reflections on the Atomic Bombs Dropped on Hiroshima & Nagasaki"* (the First version 2010, the Revised Version 2020) Translated by Noriko Mizusaki
*Participation in Japanese Anthology: *"Anthology of Asian Poems for Multicultural Symbiosis"* (In Japanese)
*Her Poetry Books Published in Japanese: *"Asian Winds" "In Front of Goya's Paintings" "Fire Festivals" "A Long Night"* and *"Love Songs"* and Others.
*Poetry Books Published in English with Italian Translations: *"Japan Sail Up" "My Thoughts for World Peace" "Admiring World Beauties"* (Published in Italy)
*Memberships: Japan Poets Club, Japan Poets Association, Japan PEN, American Literary Translators Association, UPLI/ WCP Vice President, The Poets group in California with POV Zooms, The Irish Association of Japan.
At Present, She Publishes Haiku, Tanka Poems and the Translations in *"Coal Sack Magazine,"* Quarterly and in *"The Poets Congress"* magazine, Monthly.
A Chief Editor of *"PANDORA BOOKS,"* Multilingual.

E-mail: the-mizusaki@pop21.odn.ne.jp

翻訳者略歴

水崎野里子 (みずさき　のりこ)

日本、東京生まれ。現在は千葉県に在住。世界各国へ旅行経験。海外
詩祭に英語版で参加多数。

* 翻訳・エッセイ集：『エッセイ文庫 4　英米の詩・日本の詩』『多元
  文化の実践詩考』『詩と文学の未来へ向けて』『世界の詩人たち』『家
  族の肖像』（日本語表記）
* 翻訳・編集：『現代英米詩集』『現代アメリカ黒人女性詩集』『現代ア
  イルランド詩集』『現代アメリカアジア系詩集』『現代世界アジア詩
  集』（日本語表記）
* 日英バイリンガル翻訳集：アンソロジー『原爆詩 181 人集』（共訳・
  日本語表記）第 18 回宮沢賢治学会イーハトーブ賞奨励賞受賞
* ディヴィッド・クリーガー（USA）（英語）詩・水崎野里子日本語訳
  『神の涙』（初版 2010 年、改訂版 2020 年）
* アンソロジー英語版参加編集参与：『戦争と平和詩集：10 人の現代日
  本詩人の声』（英語表記）The English Version of the Anthology（Joined and
  Edited）: "The Poems of War & Peace: Voices from Contemporary 10 Japanese Poets"
* アンソロジー参加：『アジアの多文化共生詩歌集』（日本語表記）
* 日本語個人詩集：『アジアの風』『ゴヤの絵の前で』『火祭り』、短歌
  集『長き夜』『恋歌』
* 英語版個人詩集イタリア翻訳付： "Japan Sail Up" "My Thoughts for World
  Peace" "Admiring World Beauties"（In English and Italian/ Published in Italy）
* 所属：日本詩人クラブ、日本現代詩人会、日本ペンクラブ、アメリ
  カ翻訳者協会（ALTA）国際会員、UPLI/ WCP Vice President、POV
  ズーム・カリフォルニア詩人会、日本アイルランド協会。「コール
  サック」「詩人会議」に寄稿。多言語誌「パンドラ / PANDORA」主宰。

連絡先（E-mail）： the-mizusaki@pop21.odn.ne.jp